One
Night
Stands

Rosa Liksom

One Night Stands

Translated by Anselm Hollo

Library of Congress Catalog Card Number: 93-84269

A catalogue record for this book is available from the
British Library on request

These stories are works of fiction. Any resemblance to
actual persons, places or events is purely coincidental.

First published in Finland in 1990 as *Yhden Yön Pysäkki*,
Unohdettu Vartti and *Tyhjän Tien Paratiisit* by Werner
Söderström Osakeyhtiö, Helsinki

Copyright © 1990 by Rosa Liksom
Translation copyright © 1993 by Anselm Hollo

This edition published 1993 by Serpent's Tail,
4 Blackstock Mews, London N4, and 401 West
Broadway #1, New York, NY 10012

Typeset in Great Britain by Method Limited, Epping, Essex

Printed in France by Firmin-Didot Groupe Hérissey

One Night Stands

He was born during the spring rush, at a quarter past one, in a windowless room under bright fluorescent lights. When he was three, he stopped wetting his bed and scalded his hand in boiling water. His aunt brought him a remote-control spaceship from Stockholm. He had seen one just like it in the store at the mall. At five, he looked out the window. He saw a lot of concrete and an oily mud puddle. His mother bought him a white mouse for a pet. Two months later he dropped the mouse into boiling water and it died. He fished it out with a tablespoon and flushed it down the toilet with his oatmeal. At seven, he refused to go to school after the first day. He lay in bed with his head under the pillow and pretended to be deaf. Then came winter, and he put on his skis and shuffled across the railroad bridge. With melancholy eyes he looked at the white highrise apartment buildings clustered at the edge of a field. At eight, he became an expert at lifting chocolate bars and other insignificant items from supermarkets and got away with it. At nine, he sniffed gasoline and felt his tense body relax. At ten, he set the school on fire. All it took was a little gasoline and a match. A week later he was taken to a children's psychiatric ward. There he built model *Luftwaffe* bombers and didn't say anything. On Saturday nights he was allowed to watch television until eleven o'clock. The following spring found him sitting on a rock with a bag of glue under his nose, staring at the approach of summer. The landscape was animated by laughing faces and dots of many colors. Then there was the wedding. His mother re-married. At eleven, he stopped sniffing gasoline and started using butane lighters instead. They were far more effective and less cumbersome to use. At twelve, he stole a car and drove it off the road. No one died or even got hurt. Then came summer, and he was sent to relatives in the country. The country smelled like shit and was so quiet at night that he couldn't sleep. At thirteen, he stopped using chemicals and replaced them with the cheapest brand of white wine and North State cigarettes. He bought a switchblade and threw it at the door of his room for two hours seven days a week. Autumn meant wet sneakers. He switched from white wine to vodka and broke into the burger stand at the mall. At fourteen, he drank a pint of Russian vodka and didn't even get high. He sat in the rear of the bus between Maunula and the city center and wished he would never see his fifteenth birthday. At sixteen, he committed a successful break-in at the corner store. He had enough cigarettes to last him for months, and the floor of his room was covered with stacks of chocolate bars. That winter he gave up hard liquor and switched to beer. He stopped going downtown and mostly sat in his easy chair, arranging empty beer bottles in rows. At seventeen he refused a needle he could have stuck in his left wrist. Unsmiling, he opened his ninth bottle of beer. He stopped eating and no longer watched television. He coughed like he had TB, morning, noon and night. At nineteen, he slouched, white-faced, in his easy chair and let his belly grow. He was waiting for it to be time for the autopsy and the report that would confirm the destruction of his interior organs.

That day began with a mild west wind from the sea. The fog evaporated by nine o'clock, and the sun came out, although it does provide more heat in those parts of the world where they have wars.

I got out of bed quietly, gathered a pile of butts off the filthy floor and managed to roll a smoke. I lit up and felt how the intense cold gave me goose pimples and made my nipples shrivel. Carefully, I slipped back under the covers and enjoyed the relaxing effect of the day's first smoke.

Next to the wall, Kefa was sleeping it off. Naked, reeking of sweat, his face swollen. His jaw had dropped, and a thin trail of spittle gleamed in the sunlight. He was only twenty years old. No one would believe it. I stared at his grotty face and beat-up body and enjoyed the sensation of loathing that rose up so strong it made my eyes dim. That body and face were truly uninspiring.

I hated him. I could have killed him, I could have stabbed his miserable body full of holes. I could have offed him with his own switchblade or chopped him up into steaks with an axe. But I didn't do that. I just lay there in the dim light of the stinking pigsty. I waited for him to wake up so we could go out into the sunshine and downtown to hustle up some cash for the day's first bottle of cheap wine.

My head felt like a drumful of tar, my arms and thighs

were decorated with large purple bruises, and my insides hurt. It wasn't the first time, nor would it be the last. I could count on that.

I looked at the cobwebs hanging from the ceiling and re-collected the romantic events of last night. Slowly, unemotionally, making sure I wouldn't get depressed.

Yesterday. Yesterday was like every other day, another rattling boxcar in this fucking train that was three hundred and sixty-five empty boxcars long.

We spent the day downtown, boozing, doing our usual rounds. The railroad station, the mall, the railroad station. In the evening we went to the thirteenth farewell concert of The Sleeps. I danced, and Kefa kept an eye out for fresh young pussy. By ten o'clock he'd succeeded: Lili was glued to his leather jacket.

All day long Kefa had treated me like an asshole, and things got worse as the night went on. Of course I realized that he felt I was getting in the way of his creative urges. Cramping his style with Lili. I wanted to split but Kefa wouldn't let me.

"You're not going anywhere, you silly cunt . . . You just wait here like a good piggie, then we'll go home together . . . I know you, one can't let you go anywhere by yourself, not even there." So I stayed obediently to witness things to come. But I was really pissed off.

After the concert, a bunch of us went to the guys' gym to continue the party. That night smelled of embrocation and felt that way, too. Everybody fell out after a while.

I woke up after midnight because Kefa was screwing Lili right there next to me. I thought that was a bit much, so I picked up my stuff and went out into the hall. Kefa gave me an angry stare as I left.

It was fucking cold out in the hall. I stood there for a while and then I went into the room next door where Ana and some others were sleeping it off. I fell on the couch next to Ana, leaned my head against her bony shoulder, and drifted off again.

In the morning, before anyone else was awake, Kefa came charging into the room, and when he saw me lying there next to Ana, he went apeshit. My sleep was rudely interrupted when he grabbed my hair and threw me to the floor.

He didn't say anything. I didn't say anything. We walked across town. I was wearing high heels in the snow.

I could tell from the way he looked and moved that he was full of disgust and rage. I knew he was running and re-running a movie, one in which I had shared my cunt with Ana.

The closer we got to home, the greater the pressure felt in my lungs and throat. I knew exactly what would happen after we had climbed through the window.

"Take off your coat!" he yelled.

I obeyed and stared at him without blinking an eye. I didn't try to explain or argue, because I knew that meant he'd just hit me some more.

He stood in the middle of the floor like some fucking marble statue and spat at me. He was like an animal. I didn't move. I stood there and despised him. He spat, yelled, hit and kicked me. I fell down on the floor, and he picked me up and dragged me along the walls, scraped the mortar off them with my back.

I didn't cry. I tried to protect my face with my hands. The likes of us can't afford plastic surgery.

That went on for a while. Then he collapsed, weary and satisfied. I licked my wounds for a few hours and fell asleep next to him.

We were walking on the shoulder of the freeway in the year's first heavy snowfall. The stars were tumbling down and round-bellied baby angels were jostling each other among the stars. The whole countryside was a seething white mess.

He lit a cigarette and squinted into the headlights of an oncoming car. His belly was full of alcohol and cheap West German diet pills.

"Is this reality?" he asked, in English, when the wind ripped the cigarette out of his mouth. I glanced at the sleeping village by the side of the road, lost in its friendly and sterile dreams, unaware of what went on elsewhere in the world.

Every morning when he woke up alone in his room he lit his first cigarette and used his teeth to open a bottle of beer. He stared at the white door of the closet and cursed the new day. He was determined to die from cirrhosis of the liver and lung cancer.

We returned to the village, taking the long way around. The blizzard felt powerful enough to tear out your hair, and it numbed your hands. On both sides of the road lay muddy fields, their innards bare to the sky. The swarms of seagulls that usually hung out there had flown away before nightfall.

First the streetlight vanished, then the village disappeared, and then the lights of the city, far away across the fields, went out, too. There was nothing but darkness, driving snow, and muddy fields. Tumbling stars and baby angels.

The first two weeks he sat still. He sat like an Indian chief, staring down at the ground. On the second Friday he went to the store, returned with a colorful plastic shopping bag, and shut himself into his room. At noon, I looked in. He smiled. There were two unopened bottles left.

When we got back to the house and stood in the dark hallway he said : "Three months off the coast of Greenland, surrounded by ice and drunk fishermen. Then, back ashore, well you know . . . "

He opened the door to his room. Neither one of us switched on the light. He kissed my hand and asked me to leave. I closed the door quietly behind me.

One night in early February he came to my room after three o'clock, sat down in an easy chair, lit a cigarette. He sat there in silence for a long time. I did not open my eyes. "Hanged himself on the second floor, like Joy Division," he said.

In the morning, when I woke up, he was still sitting in the chair, his childlike face lost in sleep.

Before I reached the end of the hallway, I heard dishes crashing against the kitchen walls. I opened the front door and the wind grabbed my open coat. Before I got to the far side of the yard, his window shattered, and a floorlamp and a big bunch of cassettes came flying through it. I did not turn to look but walked to my room, drank a cup of tea in the deep silence, undressed and went to bed.

I got knocked up. Shit, it really happened. I still can't see how it was possible, I'd been screwing guys for years without any precautions. I guess I thought I was lucky enough to be barren.

Wham, no period, and then this thing started growing in my belly.

I waited for almost three months, I was almost a mother. It was really a drag, everything tasted like shit, and gunk started dripping out of my tits. I even had to buy a bra, my titties got so tender.

About three months after that screw I lay on a table in an operating room, spreading my legs. It didn't feel like much anything. At that point all I wanted was for the lady in the white coat to push the anesthetic button and for the doctor to stick his tongs in there and get the whole thing over with.

It was one of those typical black-and-white Friday afternoons when I ran into Misty at the mall and she invited me for a drink at her place. I can always use a drink, and besides, that Misty's a dish.

I think that was the day I was knocked up. That's my theory, at least.

We went to Misty's place. Her mom and dad had gone out to lunch at the neighborhood tavern to celebrate their

fifteenth anniversary, so it was just the two of us. We talked
and had a couple of stiff drinks. I took a shower and put my
cruddy clothes back on. We put some make-up on in front of
the hall mirror. It must've taken us a couple of hours, our
hands were none too steady. Then we took off, really feeling
the buzz by now, and went down eight floors in the elevator
to the cool sidewalk down below.

Of course we knew where we were going. At that time,
Misty had had a fight with Pige, and I had just given Kaide
his walking papers. I guess I got drunk to drown my sorrows.
Or something, I don't know. I guess Misty just got drunk for
the hell of it, she really had the hots for Pige.

We took the bus to the railroad station, but our trip got off
to a bad start: we got kicked out after two stops. Just because
we started laying some shit on this guy with a fat neck. We
hadn't even got started, really, before he blew his top. He
grabbed Misty by the neck and was about to strangle her. I
yelled and screamed, and finally the driver slammed on the
brakes. He saved Misty's life by throwing us out.

So there we were, incredibly smashed, somewhere in the
sticks in the middle of a lot of trees. We walked to the next
stop and amused ourselves a little. It was cold and windy, so
we decided to perform a little lesbian number. We kissed
each other so our lipstick smeared, and Misty pushed her
hand into my jeans. It looked really heavy, especially to the
idiots who were standing at the stop. Their eyes were pop-
ping out of their heads. Then we really started to make out.
We were a big hit with those guys.

The next bus took us to the station. We didn't mean to
hang around there, shit, we had promised each other fifteen
times that we wouldn't even slow down at the station. But,
once again, it proved fateful.

Just as we got off the bus, Ike and Rami showed up. And that was that. Misty forgot Pige, I forgot my sorrows, and off we went.

At some point, the guys remembered a party in Käpylä, so we took the bus out there. People at the party were downing beers, and they had New York Dolls and Alice Cooper on the stereo.

So we partied for hours, and finally I just blacked out. I babbled on for a while, then I crashed. The first thing I noticed after that was that I was flat on my back in some really dark place, and also that someone was shoving himself into me. I remember closing my eyes tight and trying to forget everything.

But as soon as I managed to get things into focus a little I realized that it was Ike who was humping me. It was a relief, in a way. At least I knew the guy. But then my blood sugar went up when I realized that this asshole was banging me although he could see that I was off somewhere in the happy hunting grounds. I tried to push him off me, but he didn't budge. I gave up and let him get on with it.

Much later I realized that it wasn't just Ike who was screwing. Misty and Rami were doing it next to us, and a few more couples were at it over by the other wall. I gulped and tried to flush all the mud out of my head, but it was more than I could manage. OK, it could have been a blast if there had been some feeling involved, but there wasn't any. I still don't understand what fun Ike could have had screwing someone who had passed out. But I have to admit that it was quite a jolt when I realized that the guy screwing me that night was Ike and no one else. Ike isn't just anybody. Ike is The King.

So I lay there on the cold floor next to the rattling boiler. My legs were fucking cold, and I could see my breath in the air.

It was the same old story. Ike had been drunk for two months and smelled like it, too. He hadn't been anywhere near water for weeks, and his breath stank like the plague. Even though I can't say I'm all that different, at least I remember to wash once in a while.

What else to say. I tried to think of something totally else while Ike kept pumping. I could tell from the window up by the ceiling that a nice fall day was about to begin out there.

After Ike was done, Misty and I took off. The guys followed us but got off at the railroad station. I didn't feel too good but not too pissed-off either. Our make-up was a mess, and my head felt like a parrot house. We went to Misty's to sleep it off.

It was Misty who first realized that I was pregnant. She took me to a doctor, and her mother paid for the deal. Shit, if it weren't for Misty, I might have twins. Without her, I might not have realized that it was time to get my womb cleaned out. Missing a period or two wasn't that unusual, it had happened before, but then everything had been all right.

It was pretty amazing when they called from the health center and said well, it seems like the seed has fallen on fertile ground. But then they were pretty quick when they found out that I was only fourteen years old.

I said all right, when can you take care of it? I had decided beforehand that if the test turned out positive I would just get rid of it without further ado. I didn't even want to start counting to figure out who its father might be, since it would land in the garbage anyway.

At the health center they really got heavy about the paternity question. They claimed that it was my civic duty to reveal the identity of the child's father. I told them it was my private affair, and they should butt out.

They conducted about a dozen interrogations on my lifestyle, wanted to know what I do and think and so on. They couldn't really catch me out on anything, because I manage to keep up with my schoolwork in spite of everything, and my mom and dad are in the upper income bracket. They managed, nevertheless, to make me feel disgusted and sorry for myself and all that.

Now when I run into Ike, he acts just like before. He doesn't even say hello to me. I haven't said a word to him about the whole thing, and I don't give a shit. I know how to take care of this kind of stuff. I wouldn't want any jerks to help me out. Come to think of it, even if I had wanted to tell Ike about it, I wouldn't have dared. I can't even imagine what he'd look like if I told him. Or, yes, I can. He would have forced me to have that kid. Then he could have bragged to the other guys about having added another little Ike to the world's population. As far as I know, it would have been his third, and he would have been the champ. Twenty years old, and the dad of three miserable kids.

I had goose bumps on my thighs. Finally the lady in the white coat stuck the needle in my arm, and I drifted off into a deep sleep.

got in the back which was empty and stank of gasoline. Iron bars all around, a padded plastic seat for my warm ass.

One of them got behind the wheel and the other one was about to join me in the back but changed his mind and got in next to the driver.

This happened on the fourth of April at half past eight in the evening, in front of the Bio Bio movie house. I was hanging out with Mari and Tiia, smoking and watching people come down the steps from the previous show. People hurried to button their coats against the freezing wind.

We had bought tickets for *The Lenny Bruce Story*, and I was fingering my ticket in my pocket. We didn't mind waiting in line. For the most part, our conversation revolved around questions like why was it so hard to see the stars in the night sky above our capital.

We had met earlier that day, in town. Together, we had wandered around the main flea markets, gone to my place, demolished a pizza, talked about the universe, gone over the entire cosmos, then talked about ourselves again. For the first time in a long while.

Now we were standing there on the sidewalk, and I didn't feel cold. I thought about myself and life in general and came to the conclusion that life might not, after all, be the worst thing imaginable.

Then this guy showed up and said "All right, miss, get in the car . . . Over there, across the street." He had a big ass and looked like he was wallowing in a mid-life crisis.

He put his hand gently on my shoulder and pointed at a sad blue patrol car across the street. I was so amazed I just gaped at him. I had no idea what this was about.

"We're taking you in for questioning . . . let's go and find out what you have to tell us . . . So, let's get a move on, so I won't have to help you along," he continued before I had time to close my mouth.

He was wearing a light blue windbreaker and khaki pants with cuffs. I stood my ground and stared at him. Cops, I thought, plainclothes cops. It had been a while since they'd paid me a visit.

As always, there were two of them. The second guy was just like the first — nondescript, clumsy, and on the wrong diet.

"Listen, you can't just drag me off like this . . . You have no right to grab people off the street . . . First of all, I want to know what I'm charged with, or suspected of," I said in a confident and rather loud voice.

I had nothing to be afraid of. I had a clean sheet at that time. At least, I hadn't been caught doing anything illegal.

"Stop acting smart . . . It'll be better for you if you keep your mouth shut . . . You're not asking for *additional* trouble, are you?"

The other cop looked completely blank, just stood there like a wax doll, and the one who was talking to me inhaled his own phlegm with a nervous snort.

"Now let's just take this real easy, boys . . . No need to panic," I said. "I just want to make sure that you're not the kind of guys who grab women for their own nefarious purposes . . . Surely you understand that I, as a woman, can't just go with anybody who claims he's a policeman ?"

I managed to keep a straight face, although I came close to losing it.

The cops looked at each other. Then they looked at the crowd that had gathered around us. For a moment, a somber silence hung in the air.

I relented and decided to save the jerks from an embarrassing situation. As they knew very well, they were about to become targets of public ridicule.

"OK . . . Let's roll . . . I can walk by myself. You just follow me."

I got going and crossed the street against a red light. Looking neither right nor left, I made it to their car and stood there waiting for them. They shouted something, and as soon as the light turned green, they waddled over.

I was quite conscious of what I was doing. If I had put up some serious resistance, they would have let me have it as soon as they'd managed to drag me out of sight. I wasn't interested in getting my face battered. No thanks, not again. Besides, the whole scene was such a great set-up for a little comic interlude that I just couldn't help myself.

"You'll regret this," one of them huffed as he opened the rear door. I winked at him and waved to the girls who were still standing, open-mouthed, in front of the movie house. Everybody else had already trooped inside.

I had been "taken in for questioning" twice before, the first time when I was fourteen. It happened after some of us had been rearranging a display window in one of the downtown department stores. What we had thought of as a little prank became an amazingly long story.

Totally inexperienced in matters involving cops, I was in deep shit. They locked me up in a single cell for three days and nights. That was too much for a middle-class kid of progressive parents. My weak little psyche really took it hard. The first day I lay on my cot, paced about, and figured out what I'd say when they questioned me. No one came to see me or ask me anything. After a while, I got worried, and on the second day I cracked up. I started crying and shouting and beating on the door. I was homesick, in a panic, completely confused. On the third day they let me out for questioning. The commissar in charge laid some really heavy shit on me before we got Down to Business. He wanted to know who? what? on whose orders? My eyes had practically swollen shut, and I couldn't stop bawling. The interrogation was a bust. I couldn't get out a single word. They took me back to the cell to calm down, then brought me back again, but I was still totally paralyzed and scared shitless. I'm sure I would have told them everything real fast, just to get out and go home again, but I really was so fucked-up I couldn't speak.

They realized that I was having some sort of psychotic episode and drove me over to the Aurora clinic, where the doctors immediately put me under with an injection. I stayed there for a couple of weeks, recovering from the jail experience. Mom came to visit and brought me chocolates. I spent most of the time sleeping. They gave me pills, so that was no problem. Mom more or less understood what had happened, and once she had calmed down, she treated me right.

But then I had to go to court, and mom was ordered to pay a six thousand mark fine to the department store. She was furious, saying she couldn't believe she had to pay that kind of money to a business whose owner could afford to wipe his ass with those bills. But she was a good citizen and paid the fine. Our food intake became Spartan, and she sold my stereo and my kid brother's bike.

I still have nightmares about that first time I was locked up. Somehow, those days spell "doom" in my mind.

We drove past the sorting office at Ilmala, a large gray

building complex where I've labored many a Christmas vacation sorting stupid Christmas cards. I looked at my watch, it said ten. It was still surprisingly light outsde. Here and there new grass was sprouting among the old. Nature seemed to have stopped for a final breather before spring rushed onto the stage. I couldn't see a single bud on the trees, at least not through the window of the car.

The second time I got into trouble I was sixteen. One fine summer evening, a bunch of us went to the beach at Hietalahti to worship the sunset. We rolled joints, enjoyed our vacation and Finland's short summer. They came and arrested us and carted us off. None of us tried to run away, even though I'm sure it would have been possible to do so.

Our bunch has its principles. We have spoken up for the legalization of marihuana, many times. We didn't smoke it in secret. We thought it was the right of every human being who loves the environment and themself.

We weren't really stoned, either. We'd just had a few tokes to cheer us up. It was more like a ritual we shared. I thought we used drugs the right way, to inspire and help us regain the balance that the system has destroyed in us.

That time I stayed in for thirteen days. When I was questioned I acted cocky and snotty. I told them "everything" I thought about "the world". Later on I've wondered how I was able to be so brave and self-assured. Maybe that first time had been like a trial by fire. Ever since, the authorities haven't been able to make me beg for mercy.

I don't remember much about those thirteen days. There probably wasn't a whole lot to them. Floor, walls, ceiling. Wait, I do remember one thing that happened.

It was during the first round of questioning, on the third

day after my arrest. There were four cops in the room, one of them a woman, or at least someone who looked sort of like a woman. The main interrogator was one of those cheerful, stupid-looking daddies, and I pretended I was Nina Hagen, full of myself and sexy as hell. The cheerful fatso noticed that and smiled. He started out with questions about my circle of friends, my hobbies, my conscience, and so forth. I told him anything that came to mind. I went on and on, delighted that I could lay all this shit on them and they just had to sit there and listen to it. I responded to each question with renewed enthusiasm and made sure to start each reply with a historical consideration of the last thousand years. One of the guys kept typing as fast as he could, and did he ever look pissed off. The others sighed, glanced at each other, cleared their throats. Then, of course, they started threatening me. Once in a while they got the upper hand, backtracked, tried to get me to contradict myself, but no dice, I talked myself in and out of every trap. I kept pushing my mental "fast re-wind" button, and I used the "fast forward" as well. I was cool, and that gave me an edge. I managed to keep up this terrific front.

Then I lit a cigarette, and the interrogator told me to put it out. "There's no smoking here!" I used the marble ashtray and stared at the transvestite. She couldn't stand it and moved her gaze to the interrogator. At that moment, the door opened and in came one of these athletic uniformed guys with a big cigar in his mouth. As soon as I saw that, I told him sorry, no smoking here, it's *verboten*. That did it. The cigar-smoking muscle man lunged at me, and I found myself on the floor, smelling the whale-grease on his boots. His head wagged back and forth as he yelled: "You fucking whore, you haven't spent enough time in the hole . . . You think you can give me that crap . . . Goddamn fucking little cunt, I ought to hang you on the wall and whip your ass!"

I just lay there on the floor and started worrying about further developments, but luckily there were none. I lost a tooth in my lower jaw and bit my tongue — that's all. His boot moved away, and I lay there on the wall-to-wall carpeting like a limp slab of meat.

In spite of all my babbling I didn't really give them anything. It was all bullshit. I had decided never to involve others but to take care of myself. I let them see what I was up to, but I didn't let them under my guard.

The end result was that I was charged with one offense, smoking an illegal substance. The fine was one hundred and twenty-five marks. I winked at them when they let me go. I had preserved my honor and my pride. I was nothing if not satisfied.

We went through the lower entrance of the Pasila precinct station and straight to the elevator. Both cops stood right next to me, ready to knock me out if I tried to escape. I found that amusing. Third floor. All three of us stared at the door, counting one . . . two . . . three.

Cops really are primitive. As soon as they realize they can't get under your guard, they start threatening your buddies, your parents, god knows what. It's easy to lose your sense of proportion there, and you start imagining all sorts of stuff yourself. In the long run, incarceration is really effective. You have to have nerves of steel and cast-iron self-esteem to avoid falling into their traps. By the time of my second arrest I had already formed pretty clear opinions of this system and its values. They really weren't worth shit, as far as I could see. I knew, even then, what I would do with my life, but most of them didn't have the faintest idea.

Now, for the third time in my life, I opened that elevator door on the third floor, wondering how long my stay would be this time. Corridors to the left and to the right, shiny floors. I sat down to wait. I did not light a cigarette.

had this tremendous itch to get out of town. At
the ferry terminal, I made a couple of phone
calls to the guys and told them I was leaving for a while.
Micke gave me a long lecture about muggings and herpes. At
first, when I told him I was going abroad, he thought I was
kidding, but then I pointed the phone receiver at the terminal
loudspeaker, and he believed me all right.

I got on the ferry at half past five, well ahead of its depar-
ture time, checked my backpack and went up on deck to look
back at the city. I had never felt so free since the time when I
celebrated finishing trade school with a trip to Roskilde. It
felt like the whole world was open to me, and there was nothing to be worried or depressed about.

I thought about what things had been like, that fall. I'd had
a really shitty time at work. The pay was a joke. I had no previous experience and was so young — that's what they told
me, but I worked just as hard as some of the old bags they
employed. I had trouble with my guts, and at night I'd wake
up every fifteen minutes because I worried about being late
for work. I don't know. There was one guy about my age
there, but he was a complete idiot. He had moved to Helsinki
from northern Karelia and was so shy that he was afraid to go
to the john because he was worried the latch wouldn't work.

I was lonely as shit, all those months. I did my work quietly and well, just like a good worker should, at least from the bosses' point of view. But it pissed me off when the boss came round and praised me. The fucker positively oozed all over me in public. But what could I do. I had nothing to say to any of them.

The women who worked there thought I was queer, and so, it seems, did the boss. Once one of them shouted something like look at that kid, shakes his ass like a woman. That was because none of them had any idea of what was cool. They thought I was some kind of pervert, and I saw no reason to correct their opinions.

I baked those Karelian piroshki eight to twelve hours a day, in the sweat of my brow and armpits. So this was my dream come true? All we needed was a microwave. The more I started thinking about my hopes for a life worth living, the harder it was for me to stand there by the oven. So I quit.

I let the air stream straight into me, I "breathed sea air" the way people do in movies. I went to the store, paid for a small pack of Underberg bitters, and walked out with it *plus* a nice presentation bottle of Hennessy Cognac VSOP in a gold-colored box.

At the bar, I had a couple of drinks. That first buzz was sheer bliss.

I'm a quiet sort of guy, and I don't find it easy to make conversation with people I don't know, never mind how interesting they may look to me. But after a while this female comes up and starts talking to me. I had noticed her eyeing me at the terminal. I pretended to be interested in her stupid questions because she was good-looking and it had been a long time since I last ran into one who looked as free and easy as this one.

"So you're really into fashion, right?" she started out.

"Now that's a truly weird come-on," I said. I knew the score. All my systems were go, and I knew I looked just the way I wanted to look.

"No, but really?" she smirked.

"Come on, sweetheart, try a little harder."

We kept that up for a while and giggled a lot. The fact that she dug my style was a sign of some awareness. It surprised me totally.

She said she was really into nature and animal life. We went to the rear of the ferry to watch the sea-gulls. Then we went to the front end, to kiss and dance a little. It felt good to touch her, it had been a long time since I had last touched a woman. That job had been such a bummer that I hadn't managed to get laid since Christmas. Even jacking off gets boring if you have to do it long enough and there's no one to fantasize about.

We went down to the deserted lower level and had a nice, uncomplicated, effortless fuck. She was dynamite. She went with the flow, didn't even mention precautions.

She stayed in Stockholm. I went straight on to the train station, grooving to my tapes on the earphones and feeling totally great.

I didn't talk to anyone on the train, just took little hits off my bottle of Hennessy and enjoyed my own electricity. Outside the window black fields and the industrial slums of southern Sweden whizzed by. I remembered to thank my parents for not moving to Skövde in 1972, even though they had been promised jobs and an apartment. If they had done that, I'd probably be loafing around in a blue parka and listening to some garbage, just like the locals.

I decided to take my time to really check out Copenhagen, go to a bunch of clubs, take it easy. I planned on staying with this lady in Christiania. Not that we had anything going, I had just met her the previous summer in Roskilde. We spent a couple of days together, sort of like a kid brother with his big sister. She took me under her wing when she heard how young I was and that it was my first time abroad. She was a neat lady. She had decorated her place Indian-style, and she did some meditation every morning before making tea. I lay in bed and watched her commune with the universe. That was her style.

The train got in thirteen minutes after seven. I put on my backpack and walked through the railroad station, up and down stairs, enjoying the European feel of things. I hadn't been there a minute when some scruffy-looking guy offered me some hash. I was about to say no thanks, but then decided there was no point in putting it off: four grams for one hundred and fifty-five marks, what the hell. We made the deal, I put my backpack in a locker and sat down on a bench outside the station for a little toke to celebrate my arrival. The weather was mild, the streets were jumping. I loaded my pipe. It had been a while since I'd had any good dope. It smelled like Afghan.

I sucked the smoke into my lungs and a warm feeling flowed through my system. My heart was really pumping, doing a good job circulating the blood through my lungs. I sat there sucking on my pipe and feeling great.

I hadn't been there long before some Finnish bum showed up and asked me for a toke. He looked like he was down on his luck, so I passed the pipe to him. I was afraid he'd give me herpes or worse, so I wiped the mouthpiece on my sleeve every time he returned the pipe to me. I loaded it a second, then a third time. I decided there was no need to be mean about it, as the dope was so cheap, and it was fun to be able to smoke without having to worry about narcs.

I still can't believe I got so stoned. That bum and I kept toking until it was all gone, and by that time *I* was gone, too. My brain was still functioning, and I was quite aware of what was going on, but I was no longer able to lift a finger, not to mention move the rest of my body. No question, I was fucked up. After our final toke, the bum shuffled off, but I wasn't able to get back into circulation. My mouth felt like the Sahara desert.

I hadn't been sitting there for more than a couple of hours when the cops arrived. They started telling me to move on. In Danish. They thought I was a Dane, and I was unable to tell them anything, I was completely paralyzed. Then one of them checked my breast pocket and found my passport. They realized I wasn't one of the locals, so now they told me in English: Move On!

I didn't budge. They looked at each other and told me, in cool and precise English, that I could choose between jail or the next train back to Finland. I would have preferred jail, but I couldn't tell them that, I just sat there squinting at them. I realized that I'd lost it. They practically carried me to platform number five. According to the digital clock, the next train would leave at seven minutes to one. One of the cops stayed with me on the bench, the other guy got my backpack from the locker. At the time, it seemed like a pretty funny scene to me. When the train pulled in, they carried me inside and said have a good trip. In Danish.

I didn't wake up until we were past Helsingborg and the inspectors came to save us from foot and mouth disease.

"No meat products, no agricultural products."

No problem, but I was pissed off, and I got more pissed by the minute. Here I had paid a small fortune for a train ride. And I had spent only four hours at my destination, right there in front of the station. What a fucking drag.

I put on my earphones and cranked up the volume on my early Stones tape.

I didn't stop in Stockholm. I detest the hypocrisy of the place. I took the metro to Västhamn and spent ten hours in the ferry terminal cafeteria, waiting for the boat to leave. I had the blues, drank eleven cups of coffee, ate two cheese buns.

At nine in the morning we arrived in Helsinki. In the freezing cold I walked across Eira to Jopi's place. I let myself in with my own key, tossed the backpack on the floor. Jopi hadn't finished his breakfast, and the record player was still on. It smelled like he hadn't let any fresh air into the place for a month. I turned the record player off, picked up the morning paper, made coffee.

I met him at the café in early January, during one of those empty rainy weeks. Three evenings in a row I had seen him shooting pool by himself. On the fourth, I decided to ask him :

"Want a game?"

Slowly he raised his eyes, looked at me with suspicion.

"I don't mind."

We played for hours, without a word, hardly even looking at each other.

It was past midnight when I racked my pool cue and left. He followed me, didn't wait to be asked. First we walked along the freeway, then we turned left. He walked into my attic room where the top of his head grazed the ceiling. He stayed. We never discussed the matter.

At the time, I worked as a photographer for a mediocre Danish cultural review and made enough to get by. He went to the welfare office once a month and collected a minimal amount of money. It was enough for him. We never discussed finances.

We spent our days at home, listened to tapes, read, took naps. In the afternoons we took long walks on the other side of the freeway where there were open fields and tree plantations. Evenings we spent shooting pool at the café or, when there was a film we wanted to see, went to the movies. Both of us were fans of those claustrophobic flicks from the Forties. After the movie, we often went to the bakery by the square and ate gateaux with almond paste.

He never lost his cool. Not in the morning, not at night, nor before and after we made love. He was not particularly interested in my body, nor in his own for that matter. He preferred staring at the ceiling to busying himself in the fields of foreplay. He slept in blue bikini shorts, and I kept my t-shirt on.

Nights, when I slept like a log, he stayed awake, lying on his back and chain-smoking. Often I woke up in the middle of the night and saw him staring at me like a mad person. There were times when I was afraid that he would strangle me one night and chop up my corpse for kindling. In the morning, when I was ready for a new day, he entered the world of dreams.

The first few weeks I would ask him, once in a while, what it was he kept thinking about all night. He didn't say anything, just shrugged, looked frustrated. Conversation was not one of his habits. Factual questions would receive a brief answer, but as soon as you asked him something of a more general nature, he would just say: "None of your business."

I got to know his abrupt movement patterns and his tense body, but I never got inside his head. He never lost his cool. He controlled himself even better than he controlled the balls on the pool table. You couldn't get a grip on him. When he was in a particularly good mood he would stroke my hair lightly and say, in a low voice:

"We-ell."

After living with him for four months, I knew a few facts about him. The chapters of his personal history never emerged in any order, but I learned to interpret, correlate, and fit the pieces together.

The first fourteen years of his life he had lived on the savannahs of Africa, in the borderlands between Kenya and the Sudan. Then he had run away from home to Nairobi and had learned to deal in tourist currency, to live in the streets and taverns, to sleep in the sweaty armpits of prostitutes, and to swallow little white pills. His parents were Danes, either missionaries or commercial agents or both (the most likely case). At some point he had done time, either in Nairobi or in Denmark. Why and how long, I haven't the faintest idea.

He wasn't a boozer and seemed completely uninterested in uppers. When he turned nineteen, he downed a bottle of vodka, but it didn't register at all. Maybe he smiled a little more. Just maybe.

One night he went out to take a pee under the stars. He covered his thin body with a shirt and black pants, took his cigarettes and lighter off the bedside table, and closed the door behind him without looking back. I went on enjoying my Technicolor dreams.

He never returned from that walk.

The whole seventh floor smelled bad, and when the man unlocked the nine security locks on the door, the stench assumed nauseating dimensions. We entered a small high-ceilinged room. He re-locked three of the five locks closest to the floor. The room contained one chair which stood in the middle of a thick wall-to-wall layer of multi-colored birdseed.

"This is just the storeroom," the man said, humming under his breath. "This is nothing."

He stumbled around in the birdseed for a moment, picked up a fistful, let it trickle back to the floor.

"It's almost dry, just needs to air a couple days more."

He opened the door to a closet. In the closet stood a huge fan ; he plugged it in. A tremendous gust of wind struck the birdseed and flung it against the walls, making it spiral up to the ceiling, then cascade back onto the floor.

"This way," the man shouted, waving to me from the far side of the room.

I dove through the birdseed tornado and followed him through a small doorway into another room.

"This is my living room." He looked dead serious as he spread out his arms. He was standing in the middle of a space filled with tropical plants and trees, stamping his feet on a thick layer of black soil that covered the whole floor.

There was not a single seat or any other piece of furniture, no sign of human habitation among the trees, lianas, and soil. I stopped in the doorway. I was absorbing the moist, sweet stench into my blood, and for a moment it numbed all my other perceptions.

"Don't be shy now, come on over here, to the living room." He pointed at a small spot where the soil had been trampled flat. I sat down, and the dampness of the soil transferred itself to my skin.

"This is my living room. The bedroom is over there, under that fig-tree. I sleep really well, with my head toward the window."

He pointed to a narrow, oblong depression under the fig-tree. It was shaped like a man and looked like a grave.

"No need to cover yourself under these white suns. I don't need clothes when I'm here."

He took off his shabby sweater and pants which were streaked with bird droppings, tossed them under the window, and wandered around the room in some kind of long underwear. His bony feet sank a little into the soft soil.

"But this isn't all. Wait till you see who lives here." He opened the window and uttered weird sounds aimed at the rooftops of the buildings across the way. Like stifled cries for help, they seemed to rise from his belly and up through his larynx to fade in the calm autumn evening.

Everything was quiet. After he had kept making those noises for a while, three small brightly colored parrots flew in through the open window. He let two of them land on his shoulders, the third on his arm. He talked to them with a blissful smile and introduced them to me: "My friends — Natalia, seven years, Pierre, five years, and Claudia, nine years old." The parrots pecked his shoulders gently, pushed their big crooked beaks between his lips, cast sharp glances at him and at me. He moved them to a branch of the breadfruit tree, and four more parrots flew in through the window, one of them pure white. He addressed each one, stroked them, let them hop around on his shoulders.

"These are my princes. There are twelve of them. They are also my children, because I hatched and raised them myself. Aren't they well-behaved?"

I nodded. The man shook his head back and forth rapidly and hummed to himself. The parrots flew from branch to branch, screeching angrily when they whizzed past me.

"Please excuse us. It's feeding time."

From the eye of the ventilation storm next door, the man fetched two scoopfuls of birdseed and sat down next to me. First he ate a couple of handfuls himself, then he fed the parrots a pre-chewed mush of birdseed.

"The others are still on their Sunday outing in the park. They won't be back until late in the evening."

I looked at his old, wrinkled face, his almost colorless eyes, the old naked torso showing every bone.

"Parrots are animals. They aren't people," he said. "There's many that gets those two things confused, but I know there's a big difference."

I nodded, dodging the birdshit that was now dribbling down from climbing frames attached to the ceiling.

"We've lived in this town for fifteen years. We used to live somewhere else, but then there were only four parrots, the others were big birds. I have no reason to remember those days. They were hard. Nothing but wind and rain, no tropical forest, nothing."

After feeding the birds, the man got up, stuck his long neck out the open window and sniffed the autumn night.

"One day I'll hatch a hunting falcon and turn it into a parrot. Some might see that as revenge, but it ain't that. For me, it's a challenge, a goal in life. It's what gives meaning to my existence. Now just think about it: a falcon as a parrot. That's some notion, wouldn't you say?"

He busied himself among the plants, dusting their leaves and spreading the bird droppings onto their thick roots.

"I used to have thirty hunting falcons." He came closer and whispered: "No point in reminiscing about that, but let me tell you, parrots can't hold a candle to them." He glanced at the present company of parrots with an apologetic expression.

"They can tell that I'm talking about falcons again. Many's the time I've promised them to stop reminiscing, but what can you do, we all have to carry our personal histories with us to the grave. But parrots are just pieces of shit compared to falcons." For a moment he looked furious but then smiled again.

Night fell on the cool streets. The remaining birds arrived, tired from their flight, and arranged themselves to sleep in neat rows on the branches. The man went to sleep, too, naked in his trough under the hot fluorescent lights. I sat in his living room until dawn, thinking about the long winter days to come when sleep would be the only meaning of life.

On a foggy Sunday near the end of April I walked across the muddy yard and pushed the white bell button attached to the oak door which was decorated with massive carvings. An old woman in a gingham dress greeted me with a forced smile, asked for my coat and pointed at a white door, the middle one of three identical ones. I nodded and went in.

The large, low-ceilinged room had whitewashed walls, and the thick, unpainted floorboards smelled old and tired. I sat down behind a low glass-topped table on a baroque sofa upholstered in green, crossed and re-crossed my legs, breathed carefully. The fresh April fog was thousands of light years away.

The ceiling supported a number of huge paintings with renaissance motifs. Bared virgin bosoms competed with the pearly skin of plump baby angels. The paintings had splendid golden frames. The virgins stared at me with enticing, gentle smiles. I wondered what mysteries those smiles concealed.

There was a row of small windows through which one could see farm fields extending past the horizon to infinity in a regular geometric pattern. Winter had worn away their green, and the black soil lay heavy at the base of this landscape. Another wall was covered from floor to ceiling with solid book cases. Yellowed novels from decades ago, books on astronomy, conquests, expeditions, and many yards of works on the humanities, all shapes and sizes. The books were packed so close that it was impossible to pry one out. Large green plants surrounded the grand piano and the pillars that supported the ceiling.

The composer entered through a side door that led to a long hallway. Along that hallway were the single rooms furnished in modern middle-class style, the therapy rooms, the so-called spaces for spiritual growth. He wore a blue cotton cap and nodded and smiled at me. He came up to me and looked into my eyes, anxious and shy, as if he didn't know what to do with his hands, his deep-blue eyes.

"You came," he finally said, breaking the long silence. I nodded.

The sound of mournful Sunday church bells wafted over from the distant village. He looked down at the gray floorboards, fought back tears.

"This isn't the end of the line for me," he said. I nodded, feeling helpless. For a long time we stood there in silence, and then, as if relieved of a great burden, he took my hand and led me through a small vestibule into an even larger room with a ceiling as high as that of a church. One wall was just a big window opening onto a curiously artificial landscape. A river wound through a narrow valley between a few tall maple trees. There was a small hogback to the right, and the endless checkerboard of farmed fields began on the far side of the river.

We stood side by side in the middle of that large room. It was redolent with centuries of suffering. On the back wall hung a crucified Jesus carved out of wood. Above his head was an inscription in archaic letters, "God is Love." Along the walls were rows of baroque sofas, bunches of divans, Japanese serving tables and heavy antique wardrobes. Three splendid chandeliers hung from the ceiling. He stood with his hands behind his back and rested his gaze on the awakening landscape. His white hands were elegant and made tender by age.

It was Sunday, silence, eternity.

We returned to the first big room. The composer offered me a chair, touched my hair gently. He lit the candles in the crystal chandelier hanging above the grand piano, then sat down at the keyboard and closed his eyes. Slowly he raised his hands to the yellowed keys, and the silence became music. The notes flowed from the piano in a beautiful endless stream that gave me goose-pimples and made my heart heavy with love. His playing came from a time when life hadn't been lived yet. He played spring, the beginning of new growth and love. He played, and I loved him.

The candles cast discreet shadows on the whitewashed walls, and the shadow of the grand piano moved slowly across old Persian rugs. The room was filled with strength and love, with the eternal mystery of life.

In the middle of a slow blues passage, the side door opened, and a big-bellied man in a white parade uniform practically goose-stepped across the floor and tapped the composer on the shoulder.

"Dinner is served in two minutes. The musical entertainment period is over."

The old man played on. The chaplain in his parade uniform stared at his wristwatch, looked impatient. "Your two minutes are up," he said and grabbed the old man's shoulder, interrupting the chord, jerking him to his feet in one quick motion. I twitched in my chair and caught, for a moment, the composer's sad and helpless eyes. Only for a moment.

"Visiting hours are over," the chaplain said, martially pointing at the door with his Sunday cigar. Before I could say a word, the old man followed him to the dining room. He walked like a rocking-chair would walk, if it could.

In the entrance hall, the old woman in the gingham dress and the frozen smile handed me my coat. Night had fallen, heavy with humidity, on the dark countryside.

The dollhouse had three walls and two floors. It stood on the eye-level top shelf of the bookcase and was the first thing to receive the frosty morning's first ray of sunlight. The room was small. In the middle stood a low white bed. Under the window stood a low table covered in make-up materials and knick-knacks. And then there was the bookcase and the dollhouse in which thirteen little dolls were sleeping, each one in its own little bed.

They slept on the white bed, restless toward morning, holding each other. Both had long blond hair entangled with the other's, and their sweaty legs stuck together.

They woke up in the early afternoon. There was no point in going to school anymore. They lay on their backs, and after a while the boy's hand sought out the girl's small breasts. They made love, as they did every morning and every night. The girl handed a roll of toilet paper to the boy and tossed the wet wad into a corner.

The boy looked worried and sad. The girl's face was impassive.

The girl got up quickly, covered her skinny body with black items of clothing which she picked up from among the dustballs on the floor. The boy lay on his back and held his breath. He pondered all the mistakes he wanted to avoid in his life.

The girl put on all her jewelry, gave the boy a cold look and started dressing her dolls in their day clothes. The boy gazed at the now suddenly remote girl, so absorbed in her play, and felt sadness grow inside him and fill him entirely.

T he studio apartment on the second floor consisted of one bright room with a bathroom. They met in April, at the shopping mall, and the boy moved to the girl's place, bringing a plastic bag full of clothes and his school books. They were so young and so in love.

The girl's mother slept on the couch beneath the window, they slept on a mattress right next to the television set. They had a lovely time. The girl's mother bought the boy a leather jacket and gave them money for make-up and cigarettes.

They spent days lying in hot foam baths, made love seven times every twenty-four hours, and swore that they would love each other forever.

Then came May, and love took a hike. When the boy carried the girl from the foam bath to the bed, she was no longer willing. The boy looked angry and hopeless. He picked up his clothes and school books and threw them in the garbage chute, on his way out.

Through the open window one could hear children shouting in the December darkness. In the small room, a boy sat in an easy chair, turning the pages of a comic book printed in another country. His face wore no particular expression. He was pale, and his well-manicured fingers drummed rhythmic patterns on his leather pants. The room was hot and messy. Many weeks' daily papers littered the floor which was covered in ashes and cigarette butts. LPs and dirty clothes were piled up in the corners.

The girl lay on the bed and waited for the sickness that would free her, at least for a few days, from the suffocating thoughts that ran their circular course in her head. At six o'clock her mother came home, went straight to the refrigerator, took out some cold chicken, and ate it standing by the sink. Then she rinsed her fingers with warm water and turned on the television set for garishly colored images accompanied by carefully spoken German.

The boy closed the comic book and tossed it on the floor, next to the water pitcher. He turned to the girl, his eyes brimming with tears. The girl dug herself deeper down under the blankets and felt deep satisfaction at the thought that the end of the world had finally begun.

The room was hot and almost dark. The fuzzy images of the horror video cast colorful reflections on the gray linoleum. The girl sat in an armchair smoking a cigarette. The boy sat on the bed, motionless. Mother had gone to the country for all of July. The refrigerator was empty and the dishes lived their own microlife in the yellowish water of the sink. The girl's face was unnaturally pale. The boy seemed to be scared both day and night. The girl got out of a chair, swayed over to the boy, took hold of his foot and squeezed it hard.

"You'll never leave me and mother, will you?" the girl asked in a fearful voice. The boy, startled, said

"No,"

and pulled his foot back out of the girl's hand.

It was winter, the city's streets and sidewalks lay covered in slush. He rang the doorbell early in the morning and woke her from deep sleep. Only half-awake, she got out of bed, put on a blue dressing gown, and opened the door. He came in, took off his shoes and coat in the narrow vestibule and walked across the room to the easy chair as if he knew the way. She stood next to the phone table. All traces of tiredness had left her face. She tightened the belt of her gown and swept her long hair back over her shoulder. He lit a cigarette, gave her a sad-eyed look. Perhaps everything was as it should have been.

She went to the kitchenette and prepared the day's first pot of coffee. He went to the phone table, picked up the morning paper and looked at it. She put on a black wool sweater and a tight skirt and brushed her hair in front of the mirror in the vestibule. Then she laid the coffee table for a modest breakfast and sat down across from him. He folded the paper carefully and put it on the floor next to the armchair. She poured coffee into two small white cups.

"When did you get in?" she asked.

"Just now, on the first morning train," he said and looked at her with a slight curl to his lips. She couldn't tell whether his expression was serious or faintly ironic. He felt depressed and tired and lit another cigarette.

It was still dark outside. The yellowish streetlights reflected off the rows of cars parked in the street. The courtyard was empty. The morning's commuter traffic had not started yet.

"You still don't have a phone."

"No, I don't."

They sipped their coffee in silence. He glanced at the damp vistas outside.

"You can spend the night here."

He nodded, almost smiled. She was stating the obvious. Tall and thin, she got out of the armchair and went to the kitchenette. He looked at her pretty legs, at the way they disappeared inside her narrow skirt. She pretended not to notice his gaze.

"Here are the keys."

She handed him two keys and smiled. A stale scent of sleep and strong coffee wafted through the room.

He used the toilet, put on his shoes and coat, and left.

He returned in the evening, a little after eleven o'clock. The courtyard was as dark and damp as it had been in the morning. Everything was quiet and nothing moved except for the freeway traffic behind the next row of highrise apartment buildings.

She was sitting in an easy chair, watching the late-night movie on a small portable set. She was wearing a white nightgown, the blue dressing gown, and pink slippers. Her finely chiseled face was calm. Her hands were those of a beauty at midnight. He glanced at himself in the vestibule mirror before he went and sat down in the other easy chair. The bluish light from the television set played on the floor in the middle of the room. Its corners remained dark. He lit a cigarette and exhaled the first puff straight up at the off-white ceiling.

"Would you like to something to eat?" she asked, turning to him.

"No," he said. He looked morose and stared at the television set.

She opened her mouth to say something but closed it quickly again. They watched the movie to the end.

"You can sleep on the couch."

She got clean sheets and a blanket from the upper shelf of the closet, stretching to reach them. Immobile, he stared at her body. He had large, heavy hands. His lips were narrow and boyish. She made up the bed, closed the roller blind.

"I have to be at work at six. I'll make some coffee for the thermos, and there's food in the icebox."

He nodded and closed his weary eyes. For a moment, he covered his face with his hands, then took off his suit coat and hung it on the chair. She went to bed, leaving the blue dressing gown draped over the easy chair. He clicked off the table lamp and sat for a long while in the dark, on the edge of the couch, before taking off his clothes, putting them on a chair, and drifting off.

He woke up with a start. It was just past noon. He lay there for half an hour, waiting for his head to clear, smoking two cigarettes. It had been nine months since he had last slept so well, and his mood had improved. He dressed and spent a long time staring out into the courtyard where a woman who wore a red coat and looked impatient was watching her child stagger around in the slush. Gray clouds covered the sky from top to bottom.

He went to the toilet, washed his face, brushed his teeth. He made up the bed, none too neatly, drank two cups of black coffee, and rode the elevator downstairs. In the courtyard he passed the woman in a red coat but did not look at her. He took a shortcut to the bus stop and stood there alone in the cold wind. The bus approached slowly, skidded to a halt. The driver had to stop at every traffic light as they made their way down short narrow streets between the tall, lifeless apartment complexes. It was a ghost town, all the way down to the central square. He stared out the window and jammed his hands deeper into his overcoat pockets. The city looked only too familiar to him. Downtown, he walked to a newsstand and bought a paper. He took it to a café and leafed through it, then sat at the table, lost in his thoughts but with a determined look on his face.

Shortly before one o'clock he glanced at his watch, stopped at the counter to buy some cigarettes, then walked to a phone booth. After he had made his call he went back to the café and ordered bacon and scrambled eggs with hash browns. The owner of the café came to the kitchen door and took a look at him. He did not notice that. He ate quickly, then disappeared into the city crowds.

When he returned to the apartment after seven, she was in the kitchenette preparing a meal. He came to the kitchenette door, greeted her with an indifferent smile. She seemed irritated. They ate potatoes with hamburger meat sauce. He drank three glasses of milk.

"How are things shaping up for you?" she asked. She sounded as if she were afraid he would have to stay longer.

"They're shaping up, all right. Little by little," he said. He read her thoughts exactly.

He felt considerably better than he had felt for months. The woman pleased him, even more because she was so laconic and cool. She liked him, all right, but his somber demeanor frightened her. She knew that there was no reason to be afraid of him. They had known each other for years. But there was something gloomy about him that made her fall silent, made the apartment seem too small for two.

"You may take a shower and borrow some of Harri's clothes. I can wash yours," she said when they were done with the meal. She regarded this as her duty. The old debt had not been paid off yet, not by a long shot.

He nodded, looked pleased.

She handed him a set of clothes out of the closet. He spent a long time in the shower and came out wearing Harri's clothes. She was watching an American serial about good and evil. He smoked a cigarette and leafed absently through old magazines. The episode ended with a repulsive title tune, and she got up and washed the dishes.

"Tomorrow is Friday, I'll be home early," she said, went to the bathroom, then on to bed. He nodded and stayed in his armchair.

On Friday, she woke up a little after five. He was still in the armchair, wearing Harri's clothes, fast asleep. He looked tired even when he was sleeping.

He woke up at seven o'clock. He listened to the radio until the news was over, then got up, dressed, peered outside. The yard looked frosty and cold. He went to the toilet and shaved, studied his own face, did not like the way it looked. He would have liked it to look a little fresher and livelier. He would have liked to erase all the wrinkles under his eyes.

He went to the kitchenette and successfully made two cups of coffee. Around ten, he took the bus into town. The temperature had dropped. His toes hurt and his hands felt frozen.

Downtown, he went to a phone booth, talked for a while, and went to the café. Jaska arrived twenty minutes later.

They sat at a window table, drank beer, didn't say much.

"How long are you staying?"

"As long as it takes."

"Where are you staying?"

"At Harri's."

"Everything OK?"

"Yes."

Jaska glanced at the other's face and hands, looked doubtful.

They talked a while longer in the cold outside the bar before they said goodbye. He took the bus back to the apartment, sat in the easy chair and looked through old photo albums. He did not recognize most of the people in the pictures. He sat and waited. People were running to and from the bus stop.

At a quarter to five, Jaska arrived and handed him an envelope. He smiled and thanked Jaska who refused the offer of a cigarette and a cup of coffee and left, looking downcast.

She came home after six and pulled a bottle of Bacardi out of her shopping bag.

"In honor of your visit!"

He was amused but didn't let on.

"I'll be leaving on the morning train," he said while sipping his first drink. "Jaska has arranged everything."

"When do you get out?" She swallowed, painfully.

"In April, and then I'll leave the country. Jaska's fixed me up with money and tickets. I got them today."

It grew darker in the room. Tobacco smoke drifted slowly toward the kitchenette.

"You see, Harri asked me to do everything you asked for . . . " She fell silent for a minute. "I got a letter from Harri. He may get out in June."

"You don't have to do anything. This was a matter between friends. Today I'm helping Harri, serving half of his sentence, but who knows — tomorrow Harri may have to help me . . . "

Now she looked even more embarrassed. They sat there silent for a long time, lost in their thoughts. She felt desolate. She had to prepare herself to live the greater part of her life alone, even though she had married a man she loved.

"I'll help you anyway, if there is anything you need," she finally said, breaking the oppressive silence.

He nodded, cleared his throat.

They finished the bottle, talked about the old days, watched a late-night soccer match.

The next morning he woke up before her, exchanged Harri's clothes for his own, shaved. She made coffee.

"We may leave the country, too," she said.

"Harri will know what to do, soon as he's out in the street again," he said and walked to the door.

"See you in April," she said as he opened the door.

He glanced at her with a look of melancholic irony and closed the door carefully behind himself.

offed him, man. I stuck him like a pig. I didn't feel any pity or disgust at all. I offed him, man, and I didn't even run away. I stayed right there, because I wanted to be in on the grand finale. Just stood there like a fucking flagpole, till the ambulance got there and took him away. Him and me, too.

He was wearing this blue jacket and corduroy pants. Nerdy, like. A blond, with those little whiskers. And *boom*, he just laid there on the sidewalk, with the juice running out of his belly. Like a puddle of nail polish. For a minute there, I didn't quite get it. I was out of it. See, that's what it felt like at first. It was like I had just happened on the scene, just stopped to look, see what happened. It felt real weird. He just laid there, didn't say a word.

Now the whole thing seems ridiculous to me. That the guy could just croak like that. If it was that easy to off me, I would have died when I was a baby. Man, the hassles I've survived. And he goes and dies from just one little stab. I didn't even hit him straight, my aim was off.

I think it was in his stars. It was like his *fate* to croak, and I just happened to be there to help him get it over with.

That he croaked like so easy just *proves* that it was time for him to go. I think it proves he was too *weak* a type to go on living. He couldn't have taken this shit much longer anyway.

So you could say I helped him escape from the treadmill. No more pain. I'm sure things weren't all that great for him. Queers can't be happy. They're incurable.

Faggots have always pissed me off. Long as I can remember. I can't understand how guys can *do* those things. It makes me puke. Shit, I can see why Adolf stoked his gas ovens with creeps like that. They should get rid of all of them so people wouldn't have to see them in the street. A man has a right to punch queers in the mouth. They ain't *human*. They're mad. I didn't kill a man, I killed an animal. A pitiful, tortured animal, that's all it was. He wasn't even a woman. You hear what I'm saying? He was just an ANIMAL. One of Nature's mistakes.

Any regular guy would have done what I did. Who can *stand* to watch that shit! Drunk or sober.

And listen, man, I don't want my mom or my stepdad to be mixed up in this. I won't let them run my childhood backward and forward. I won't plead any mitigating circumstances. I don't need any understanding or therapy. I want them to throw the book at me, and I'll do my time with pride and honor.

I've asked them to put me away for eight years. I'll be twenty-seven when I get out.

No regrets, man. I don't accuse anybody. Least of all myself, my family, or the system. I knew what I was doing. AND I DID THE RIGHT THING.

T he girl wore a rigid half-smile and a tricolor tattoo on her right arm. In the small hours, they walked through the city and its obligatory fog. They passed a man with a severely bent frame. They stopped for a moment on the bridge. The yellow lights of the coal harbor rose higher than the invisible stars.

The girl's small room was furnished in Japanese style, everything pristine and white. There was a bed, a triangular chair. A judo outfit hung on the wall. The girl prepared a foam bath. The boy sat on the chair, hiding behind his thoughts. Water rushed into the large white tub and a tall green mountain of foam rose above it. The girl undressed in front of the boy, dropped her heavily studded belt on the floor, peeled off her tight black outfit. She stared at the boy and noticed how uncomfortable he was. With her breasts, strong arms, firm thighs. Motionless, he sat on the chair and looked down at the floor. After eight o'clock she came out of the bath, didn't use the towel, walked to the bed making foam-green tracks on the floor. The boy was still sitting on the chair. Furious, she pulled the covers over her head.

When I woke up the first time it was already light. It was raining gently, droplets hit the window and ran down in narrow streaks. The last sodden yellow maple leaves fluttered down to the wet pavement. A crow flapped clumsily in the distance between the apartment buildings. It was quiet the way it is on Sunday mornings.

He went on sleeping for a long time, holding me, his nose nudging my neck. His breathing was regular and his long hair spread over my shoulders, all the way down to my small breasts. Sleepy-eyed, I contemplated the white-washed wall with its life-size poster of Marlene Dietrich. I let time go by and my thoughts change from black and white to color and back again to black and white.

A little before nine he woke up with a start. His thin lips met mine in a gentle kiss, and he held me tight for a moment. Then I felt him get out of bed and leave the room. I dressed, lit a cigarette. Sounds of loud splashing came from the bathroom. There was no one in the street down below.

I picked my cigarettes and ashtray off the table and went to the bathroom. He stood in the middle of the floor, drying himself, smiling. His blond hair fell down to his shoulders with their delicate tattoos of piano keyboards. I leaned against the doorjamb and enjoyed the view. I loved looking at him, just looking. He knew he was beautiful and how to show himself to his best advantage.

He hung the towel on the drying rack, got in front of the big mirror, brushed his hair. He looked at himself from different angles and smiled at me in the mirror. Then he opened his make-up kit, placed the jars in a neat row below the mirror, and began. He splashed warm water on his face and let the tap run at a trickle. Then he squeezed shaving cream onto the fingertips of his right hand and spread it on his face with light, glancing strokes. He winked at me in the mirror. I lit another cigarette. He took a black double-edged razor and started high above his cheekbones, pulling off the foam in long, light strokes. He rinsed the blade under the tap, then shaved the left side of his face, careful not to damage a small brown mole, and then his chin. He rinsed his face quickly with cold water, dried it with a small towel. I put out my cigarette, shifted my weight. He splashed some fragrant after-shave on his face, rinsed his hands, walked past me swinging his hips and pecking me on the cheek. I followed him back into the other room. He put on blue shorts, a black shirt, and black leather pants, then went to the small mirror and attached five earrings of different sizes to his ears. He put seven rings on his well-manicured hands, fluffed his hair with a careless gesture and left the room. I sat in an easy chair and sighed a little. Sunday mornings were always so slow. I read an English-language comic book and went back to the bathroom.

He was sitting in front of the mirror and making up his face with firm and precise strokes. Eyelashes, corners of the eyes, eyelids, lips. Everything looked right. He backcombed his hair, then used a whole lot of fragrant hairspray on it. I put out my seventh cigarette and smiled.

He walked past me, gently stroked my hand as he did so. In the vestibule he put on three belts and slipped thirty bracelets onto his left arm. Glanced into the full-length mirror, turned and came over to me.

"Time for coffee," he said and took my hand.

My mother gave birth to me on a bathroom floor in the middle of the summer while her parents were vacationing in Greece. My father, acting as the midwife, had dragged their nice spring mattresses from the bedroom into the bathroom so that my mother could give birth to me in the squatting position. She had filled the tub with boiling water to make the bathroom warm and humid. She was sixteen, my father seventeen. Her belly was so small while she was carrying me that even the neighbors didn't know she was pregnant.

I was born in the early hours of the morning, and my father bit off the navel cord and tied it with strong yarn. Entering the humid atmosphere of the bathroom, I did not cry the way babies normally do. I didn't make a sound, and my father, frightened and worried, grabbed my feet and held me upside down the way doctors do, until he had made me cry. I was born with a white caul, and my mother was horrified, afraid that she had given birth to a mongoloid or an astronaut. By midday, my father had scratched the membrane off me with the sharp nail of his index finger. Reassured, my mother lay on top of the mattresses on the bathroom floor, and my father sat on the toilet and held me in his arms. I was naked and blue.

My mother had long black hair, and she was the size of a twelve-year-old. She smiled a lot, never said much. Spilled tea on the table and wiped it up with the hem of her black gown. My mother always dressed in black. It is a festive color. My mother was beautiful, the way all mothers are, at least in their children's eyes. I have inherited her large and lively eyes. I have my mother's gaze.

My father was as thin as a blade of grass. He had a straight nose and a pretty neck. My father was even more childlike than my mother. He did not believe in himself — nor in anybody else, for that matter.

When I was an infant, we were always on the road. I never had just one home, I had dozens of them. We traveled from one country to another, one city to another, one village to another, lugging two large suitcases that contained all we owned, and the baby carriage, my domain. We slept by the roadside, in shelters, in houses, buses and trains. Sometimes we stopped for six months or so somewhere in the Portuguese countryside, among people who were handsome and kind. Father worked as a fisherman, mother drew up horoscopes for people. Everything was great, but then we had to leave again. My father became restless and we hit the road. We traveled down for the winter, up for the summer. In the summers, my father did well up there, but as soon as the first signs of fall appeared he was no longer able to sleep, not in the dark of night nor in the light of day. After he had stayed awake for two weeks and started talking incomprehensible stuff, my mother packed our bags and the carriage and we set out for the south. On the way, my father fell asleep, and everything was all right again. My father curled up under my mother's arm, the way I used to when I was small, and mother rocked him to sleep. She told me to be quiet and find my own food. I understood and threw no tantrums.

Then she had another boy. This happened when I was three, a smiling little longhair, able to charm everybody in two seconds, no matter what country or town we were in. My kid brother was born in the South of France, high up in the mountains, and I was there for the whole event. My father, Michelle, and I were his reception committee. My father was throbbing with happiness, my mother was hot from her labor, and after that birth I loathed her because she had turned so ugly and yelled and cried so much while pushing my kid brother into the world. My father had explained it all to me, but I had a hard time forgiving her.

Then spring came, and we had to start traveling north.

At the age of three, I spoke four different languages, mixing them all up. No one but my mother could understand me. Then I stopped talking for a whole year. When I got my speech back, it was my mother's. I started to talk clearly and a lot. I talked from dawn to dusk, exhausting my parents.

When my mother turned twenty, she began to regret her lost youth. She wanted to fall in love and settle in some pretty house with a man who wouldn't be as weak and restless as my father. She left, taking my kid brother along. I stayed with father who was paralyzed by grief. I was four years old and tried to help him shape up but didn't succeed for very long. He stopped sleeping and babbled incessantly — incomprehensible stuff about soldiers, nuclear wars, automobile races, star wars, and lost astronauts. I listened but couldn't understand a word. Arise and take up thy bed, he told me. I don't suppose he really knew what he wanted to say anymore. Day and night he talked, in an even, uninterrupted stream. His words filled the room, flowed out through the cracks around the window frames and in the door, filled the yard and and grew into a tall slab against the stars.

Then he started wielding an axe. He seemed to want to break down all objects into their original components, and to crush everything that moved. At that point, I ran over to the neighbors, and the men came and tied my father to a tree until the ambulance arrived and took him away. I stayed with the neighbors and did not hear anything about him for a long time.

Then my mother came back. She had found a strong, good-looking man who would be our new father. I loved him, and so did my kid brother. He was irresistibly skillful and as gentle as a bowl of warm wilk. We lived in a small village and had a wonderful time. We had happily forgotten our old father when he walked in one day, then sat at the end of the table, poker-faced, for two days. My new father tried to make friends with him, but it was no use. Father wouldn't even pick us up and hold us on his lap. His return made me feel bad. It was the first sign that things had not come to a happy end. My father was a bird of ill omen, bringing bad things and grief to my mother.

On the third day, he perked up and finally understood what had happened: there was a new mother, a new father, and a new, better life. He couldn't stand it, he did not want to share our happiness. He got up and left. That night, he set our house on fire. We were all saved except for my father who had doused himself with gasoline. And so it was that my real father burned to ashes. We grieved for a while, and then we forgot him, because our new father combined in himself all the good traits of our old father. We traveled as before but everything was calmer. Our new father was more like a real father. All of us could curl up on his shoulder, even mother. My new father was a handsome man, a pretty face, a strong body. I would have liked to grow up to look like him, but my blood is different, and I can't change that.

My kid brother Bombadil grew up to be a bright playmate. I raised him to be a warrior because that's what I always wanted to be. I was proud of him, and we spent all our days together. Once we broke into an old man's house. Bombadil was three and I was six years old. We broke a kitchen window and climbed in. Everything was clean and tidy in there. We turned on the television, it snowed and played snatches of music. We sat in the kitchen and drank cold cocoa from glass bottles. Then Bombadil opened the door of the china closet and cleaned out a shelf with a sweep of his hand. We laughed. I did the same thing. I climbed up on a chair, then up on top of the sink, and tossed plates to the floor. Then, the pantry: we poured sugar, flour, beans, and ketchup all over the broken crockery. We escaped through the window, leaving the television hissing away in the living room.

The rest of the afternoon we played Robin Hood and giggled in the woods. When we came home, mother was in tears. She didn't hit us or say anything, just cried, bitterly. I realized that our misdeeds had been discovered. I felt ashamed. The next day I went back to that house and handed the old man a sea-chart I had stolen. He looked at me with sad eyes and turned away. I felt such remorse that I could have climbed a tree and thrown myself down into the heather.

Once a week, we went to a big communal sauna where large old folk of both sexes sat on the benches, drowsy, chin on chest, stroking their layers of fat, exchanging half-asleep smiles in the scorching heat. I observed how the old women's breasts hung down empty and how the old men's penises had disappeared somewhere behind the third roll of fat. Mother washed me and my kid brother, and father washed mother. Wearing her heavy string of beads, mother sat on the bench to the right, father facing her on the opposite bench. They looked admiringly at each other and at us. My brother and I sat in a large brown plastic basin in the middle of the floor, in front of the stove, and used little dippers to splash water from the basin onto the floor. Since I couldn't stand having my hair washed, I was often afflicted with headlice that made my head itch painfully. After the sauna we put on clean clothes or else the ones we had been wearing, inside out. Then we went to the café close by and drank cold cider through a straw.

My new father was fair and good-natured, just the way my old dead father had been. They were very similar, at least in their positive traits. My father rarely made money, and we lived off the scraps of others, gathered by my father from the large dumpsters of big city supermarkets. We always had fruit and vegetables at home, and on weekends my father brought all kinds of delicacies to our table. On his rounds, he would come across whole crates of cheese or bags of plums, sometimes even old sunglasses. It was like Christmas. In the summers, my father went fishing, and in the autumn we gathered berries and mushrooms.

Once, in the middle of winter, when my father became

keenly aware of the world's injustice in the distribution of wealth and dwellings, he took me and my brother into the village. We went to the nicest house in the whole village, there was never anyone in that house at this time of the year. We went in through the verandah window and my father switched on the central heating. This is our home now, he told us with a smile. In the wonderful warmth, we took our clothes off and chased each other through the rooms. Father listened to Stravinsky on the stereo, smoked a cigarette, made some Italian coffee and gave us drinks of soda water. In the evening, mother came to get us but we didn't want to leave. I couldn't understand why mother didn't like our great new home. Father sat in an armchair and told mother that this was only right and proper. Mother looked worried and said something about the neighbors but finally agreed to stay and have some Italian coffee with father.

We slept in the nursery, in great big baroque beds, and mother's and father's bedroom smelled of lavender. A couple of days later the police came, took father away, and chased us out into the street. We went home with mother and lit a fire in the stove. Father returned the next day. He was in a good mood, he had been sentenced to a fine which he did not intend to pay. All of our farts smelled the same: black rye bread and butter. We ate that rye bread in the morning and in the evening and drank many pots of tea during the day.

Once, when we were living in an old wooden cottage, father brought Bernard home. Father had found him downtown, in front of a large mirror in a department store. Bernard and father were old friends. When they were kids they had played World War Two together. Bernard had spent many years in the hospital, in the psychiatric ward, but father had never gone to see him there. Bernard stayed with us for weeks. He sat stiffly on his chair and smiled all the time. His teeth were yellow, and there were flecks of white foam at the corners of his mouth. Mother talked calmly to him while she was cooking. Bernard did not reply but went on smiling.

I often sat on his frozen lap, marveling at his smile and his eyes that were just slits. Then, one day, father said he was taking Bernard back to the hospital, even though that wasn't the ideal thing to do, but there was no way Bernard could go on staying with us.

They walked off to the bus stop, Bernard with short abrupt steps. I haven't seen him since, nor have I ever asked my father about him.

About half the time, mother and father didn't know where we were headed. They would visit for days with friends along the way and tell us to go and amuse ourselves. So I would ice-skate or roller-skate in icy courtyards, never bothering with mittens or hats, always feeling cold. My kid brother sat on a sled in the yard and clapped his hands, no doubt hoping he'd grow up to be as big and skillful as me.

One summer we climbed a tall mountain somewhere in southern Spain. We had started out from the valley early in the day and spent all morning climbing this really steep slope. At first, I managed to walk, then I rode on father's shoulders (branches of small trees and bushes painfully scratching my face and bare feet), then I walked again. It was exciting to climb that narrow path ascending straight to heaven. We had to grab hold of rocks and roots to keep going. Father said it was not a good idea to look back, but I kept glancing over my shoulder at the village as it became an ever tinier dot down in the valley. Just as we reached the summit, in the afternoon, a wind rose and it began to rain. The summit was a long, narrow, perfectly level plateau devoid of bushes or grass or rocks. A level stone floor.

From up there, we saw the blue waves of the sea, the tiny village, an endless horizon. On the far side was a gigantic reservoir and a huge dam with a highway running across the top.

It looked strange.

Father said that this was all man-made — that we had spent the whole day climbing up the wall of the dam.

The rain was warm and the wind blew hard. We ran onto the edge of the dam and took shelter behind some roadside flowerbeds. After a while. a bus came and took us back to the valley.

I never found out that girl's name nor where she was from or where she went. I was at the market with my mother, gathering vegetables off the pavement and saving good pieces of fruit from the cleaning trucks, when I saw the girl sitting in a doorway. I stared at her and she smiled at me. I ran to her and jumped straight into her arms. She kissed my cheek and squeezed me tight against her small breasts.

Then mother came and had a long conversation with her. Mother asked her to visit, and she came.

She had long red hair decorated with animal bones, feathers, and brightly colored beads. All evening we played prince and princess and neither one of us got tired of the game. Late at night we had parsley tea and ate potato pancakes mother made. I fell asleep in the girl's lap, she stroked my hair, and I had lovely dreams.

When I woke up the next morning, the princess had left. I didn't feel sad, just let my love rage all over the bedroom.

Once father borrowed a motorcycle from some bearded friend of his. We packed two small backpacks and tied them securely to the small rack. Father started the bike and I sat behind him, holding on tight to his thick leather jacket. We drove through the village and through town, and I leaned my head back as far as I could. Father drove fast and I screamed and had a great time. The highway smelled of burnt asphalt and oil. When father stopped at filling stations, I took a pee, drank soda water and played space invaders. Father checked the pressure in the tires, and off we went again. I pretended I was an astronaut in a distant galaxy. Inside my helmet the world felt very small. At nightfall we'd stop and camp by a lake or by the edge of the woods. We made a fire and fell asleep, close together, under the stars.

A present I remember was this tiny little walkman a friend of mother's brought me from America. It was used but worked perfectly: play, re-wind, fast forward. It came with an Italian fairytale cassette, and I listened to it dozens of times, imagining that the little machine contained a small Italian theatrical company, a group of wonderful little fairytale people from Rome.

My father told me it was just a machine, there was no life inside it. I believed him, yet I kept on imagining what kind of life those little people led who spoke a language that was foreign to me. The batteries wore out soon, and mother got tired of buying new ones. In spite of all that I carried that Italian world with me for a long time. I kept the machine clipped to my belt in the daytime, and at night I stuck it under my pillow. Sometimes when I felt sad, I imagined myself into the machine and was able to forget my sorrows.

Once, father went to work in another country but promised to return the following summer. Summer came but father didn't show up. Mother became sad and cold. We lived in a small room, and regular meals became a thing of the past. I just about managed to make tea for us in the mornings. I whined and bothered my mother, and my kid brother started wetting himself. We were cruel and made mother cry, but when she started crying I got frightened and jumped into her lap and consoled her with every nice word I could remember.

Then father came, at the very end of summer. He had a lot of money because he had been working at a big fish cannery and had also been dragging fish out of the sea with huge nets. He took us to the zoo. They had a lot of animals there, and even more people. We walked from one cage to the next and tossed peanuts to the reindeer. Then we saw a Siberian tiger. There was a fence and shatter-proof glass between him and the public. Father climbed over the fence and put his face right up against the glass. Bravely he stared the tiger in the eye. The tiger didn't budge, just gave the glass a lazy lick of his tongue. All the kids applauded, and I shouted as loud as I could that that was my father.

We were sitting in a train somewhere between Istanbul and Bucharest. The train was crowded, even the aisles were packed with people. It was June, and sweat ran down my back onto the plastic bench and made the seat of my pants wet. I sat next to the window and looked at the yellow corn-fields, at the white villages, at the sun that drilled its light through the countryside. There were twelve of us in a compartment designed for eight. Ten grownups, my brother, and me.

Across from me sat an old big-bellied man with a small

round skullcap. He kept glancing at a woman in a yellow skirt who sat at the other end of the bench. She was wearing a necklace of bright green plastic beads and white patent leather shoes. She looked like a Yugoslav whore to me. She looked at the man and he looked back at her. The other passengers pretended not to notice. After the next stop, they went to the back of the carriage and stood next to an open window, chatting and smirking at each other.

After a couple of hours they came back inside, and the people who had borrowed their seats had to get up again. The woman sat down next to the fat man and looked very small and nondescript there. The other passengers disguised their curiosity and looked down at the floor. I stared at the woman and saw how the man's left hand was groping one of her big tits.

In the middle of the winter we lived in a roomy two-story house that had a big open fireplace. I constructed little houses out of paper and cardboard and put them into the fireplace until I had a nice little town in there. I attached the houses to the hearth with candle wax and dripped some more candle wax onto their roofs so that they looked like they had snow on them, and so they would burn longer. When it was all ready, I set fire to a corner of one of the houses, and soon the fire spread from one house to the next and to the fences and the church steeple. Whenever the fire went out, I rebuilt the burned houses and started another fire from another corner. I stood and watched the lovely little flames and tried to guess which houses would survive the fire undamaged. I enjoyed this game for weeks, and Bombadil sat in front of the fireplace and watched it with an ecstatic expression. Then I decided to make the houses a little bigger, using milk cartons and yoghurt containers. I covered these with colored bits of paper and cut out windows and doors that you could open and close. I burned everything down and carried the ashes to the kitchen stove. One afternoon I got tired of my town planning and building and decided to give it up.

From the fireplace I moved on to the bathroom. I filled the tub with water and launched a model liner I had built. I took some nail polish remover from the bathroom cabinet and splashed it over the deck. Bombadil stood next to me with the hand-held shower head, wearing a fireman's helmet, ready to act if the fire on board ship went out of control.

I set fire to the ship. In a few seconds, the plastic melted into a shapeless lump. The bathroom filled with black smoke and the acrid smell of burnt plastic. Bombadil tossed the shower head into the tub and we ran out into the yard. It was quiet in the yard, just as if nothing had happened.

One summer we lived in London or rather in a small suburb of that city. A friend of my mother's had given us the use of his apartment while he was in Africa. Father worked on his motorcycle in the yard, and mother worked as a mail carrier in the mornings. Across a little hill was an old railroad station where local trains arrived every hour from central London. I was dreaming about a trip round the world. I had mentioned it to my mother many times, but her response always consisted only of a tolerant smile.

One morning, while mother was distributing mail and father was asleep. Bombadil and I crept downstairs. We stuffed two sweaters and some gloves into a backpack, walked to the station and caught the first train. It was not one of the yellow suburban line trains. For a long while we sat on the soft seats and stared out the window at the suburbs flying past.

When the conductor came and asked us for our tickets, I proudly handed him an old crumpled local train ticket.

"Where are you going?" the conductor asked.

"Around the world," I said, full of enthusiasm.

The conductor stared at us, and so did our fellow passengers. That train was on its way to Liverpool. We were taken off the train at the next stop, and the police drove us back to our station. I had refused to give them our home address.

Bombadil giggled because the police looked so disgruntled, and I told him that any first try was liable to go wrong. We decided not to feel discouraged. It was late when we walked home with the police following us. Father and mother had just sat down to supper, quite unperturbed, but pleased when we showed up. The police explained something to my father, and he thanked them and showed them the door. We had macaroni and went to bed early.

Last summer we spent five months in Greece. It is always warm there, and the people are friendly. The sea makes mighty waves, and father even lets me have some wine when there is a festive occasion, which is quite often.

While we spent the previous winter in the countryside, mother had made costumes for twenty characters, and my father built sets and composed music for the saxophone. We put on puppet performances in the Athens marketplace, and Bombadil passed the hat. Sometimes we had a big audience, sometimes just a couple of penniless kids. All day tourists came by and took pictures and gave us money. Father played the saxophone or sang and played the electric guitar, and mother and I did the costume changes. We spoke the parts in English, but that didn't seem to bother anybody. After the performance, mother gave me a hug, and we went to eat in some cheap taverna. Father always ordered a large beer.

My dad bought me this apartment in Eira, it wasn't cheap, but back in Haukilahti we had these constant fights about hygiene. There was dust everywhere, and god, you should have seen the bathtub. I had to disinfect it every single time I used it. I couldn't use the toilet before spreading a sterilized cover on it. We had fights every second, and so he bought me my own crib. It's a nice one, great high ceilings, it's been renovated from top to bottom. So I moved in here and breathed a great big sigh of relief that I wouldn't have to spend all day cleaning up the place. But on my second day here it occurred me that the previous inhabitant might have been some incredible queer or something, so I went and bought some heavy-duty cleansers and spent three weeks on the job. I even used a toothpick to clean out every nook and cranny, and finally the place looked real good. Then I started thinking I should get a job. I spent a couple of days trying to figure out what it was I wanted to do, but then I suddenly noticed the windowsills. Christ, they were positively grimy, god knows what pollutants I may have in here. So I just had to forget about job-hunting and get down to scrubbing again. I started cleaning the place and had no time for anything else. Luckily, Dad brought me food from Stockmann's every day, so I didn't have to tear myself away and go out. I trust

Stockmann's, all right, but there was one big problem with Dad's visits. You see, he's a business man and flies all over the world — shit, can you imagine what a bunch of diseases he may be the carrier of? Without even knowing it himself. So every time Dad came to visit I had to disinfect everything he touched. That was it for the summer, I didn't get out of the place even once. Well, I couldn't, could I, it was so filthy and dirty out there. Then, on the first of September, Mari came back from Greece. She'd dressed up all in white because she knows how important cleanliness is to me. At first, everything was OK, but then Mari wanted to kiss me, and that gave me the dry heaves when I thought about the diseases she might have caught. So I told her "later" — after she'd taken a shower and disinfected herself. When Mari came out of the bathroom I touched her hand and kissed her, but then I remembered that AIDS is spread through French kissing, and I really panicked. I asked her to swear she'd been faithful to me, and she swore she had. In the evening, Mari went back to her place and left a bottle of Greek wine she'd brought me as a present. I poured it down the toilet, disinfected the toilet, and went to bed, but I couldn't sleep. I kept feeling this urge to clean all the places Mari had touched. So I cleaned house until five and slept the whole next day. Mari brought me some warm food from Stockmann's after she got off work and told me she wanted to spend the night and make love to me. I told her I couldn't make it with a woman who had just come back from Greece. I explained to her that we should wait a couple of months or so, and if she didn't show any symptoms by then, why, no problem. Mari agreed and went home like a good girl. Luckily she didn't have time to sit on more than three chairs, so I was done cleaning them by midnight. So the fall passed, no change, Mari brought food and Dad came and checked that everything was all right. No one said anything about my getting a job, myself least of all, because it was clear to me that I couldn't have held down any kind of job in addition to this continuous house-cleaning. Nor could I imagine working in some slimy office with several people breathing the same air and all. At Christmas time Mari and I considered making love, and I was almost ready but changed my mind at the last moment, just to be on the safe side. In the spring, we got married because Mari wanted us to, and Dad did, too. A clergyman came to my place to marry us, and Dad gave me a set of dumbbells as a wedding present. After the wedding I cleaned up the place and started working on my muscles. Mari was real impressed when she saw how big they were getting. She still came, once a week, and brought me enough food for the week. Luckily, her visits grew shorter every time, and she no longer said anything about making love. I worked out and cleaned house all day. After a year my biceps bulged even when I relaxed, and my thighs were like two icebergs, I kid you not. Mari stopped coming, and I'm glad she made that decision, I can do without all that extra cleaning. Mom and I haven't seen each other since I moved out from Haukilahti, but Dad has really shaped up great. Now, when he comes to see me, he pulls plastic covers over his shoes and puts on a white coat and a sterile face mask and a pair of those disposable plastic gloves.

This started before I turned eighteen. I sat in an easy chair in the living room and watched my mother prepare food in the kitchenette. That was when I realized it for the first time. All of a sudden I felt sick as shit, and this lightning-bolt ran through my brain, and I saw her there in the kitchenette as some kind of mutant, as a parody of a human being. I'm sure that was when it started. Over the years I have merely become more convinced that I was quite right about that, even back then, as a kid. I hate all women. I hate every woman who walks toward me in the street, in the park, out in the fields or in an office corridor. I get goose-bumps when I have to look one of them in the eye or exchange amiable sentences with her. But I do it, all right, I have even become good at it over the years. I make small-talk, no problem, I even smile at strange women, but this does not ease the feeling of hatred and revulsion that overwhelms me in such situations, not one bit. I am ready to remove each and every living woman off the face of the earth. I would like to establish a kingdom of men, sufficiently large, with well-defined borders and abundant natural resources, where Penis Power decides everything. The bigger the penis, the greater the authority. Women are disgusting and primitive, even from a scientific point of view, with our slimy cunts, bleeding orifices, gaping mouths, and stinking armpits. That is the truth about us, and that is why I have been working on a new law under which, as of next year, all newborn females will have their throats slit immediately, in the maternity ward, where this can be accomplished in a manner both hygienic and efficient.

have been living with my mom for eighteen years, just her and me. When I was born, my dad had already split, and we never made much of an effort to find him. I never missed him, and I don't think I would have had any use for him. I have shared everything with my mom since I was a kid. During puberty, when kids tend to have problems with their parents, we got along even better. Mom has never gone to work. She was always at home when I was little, and I really enjoyed that. Others were dragged off to day-care or relatives, but I could always stay with Mom. For these eighteen years, if not longer, Mom has been on disability. I guess she had a bit of mental trouble when she was younger, but I must say I've never noticed anything odd. I'll admit that she's always been a little on the quiet side, a bit shy, and she's never liked going outside much. As soon I was able, I started taking care of the shopping and the lottery tickets and things like that. We always got along great. We always watched TV in the evenings, sometimes we played cards, and at least once Mom tried to read to me from some fairytale book. She crocheted afghans and sold them to Gypsies to make a little money. She gave me that money immediately and told me to buy whatever I wanted. We lived on the sixth floor and had a great view of the tower of Malm fire station. We would make bets as to when the sirens would go off and the red beacon start blinking, and then we'd try to guess where the fire was, and how big it was, and the next day we checked the papers to see who had come closer. Mom was really cute, a slight little thing, really fair-skinned and agile, even though she wasn't quite as thin as I would have liked her to be. I always came straight home after school and hardly ever hung out with the guys in the yard. I just wasn't interested, I never cared for that gang stuff. I am a quiet sort of guy and have always liked it at home. I finished school with reasonable grades, even though I had been the butt of my schoolmates for all those years. Mom would console me when I got home. I didn't give a damn about those kids, I was more mature than all of them put together, but I decided there and then that I wouldn't pursue school beyond what was obligatory. Mom thought that was all right, too. I got a job with the post office, and she was real glad about that, since it meant security and a pension. Everything was really hunky dory. But then, when I came home from work one night, Mom had already gone to bed. I thought that over for a bit, it seemed strange for her to be in bed so early. I couldn't remember her ever going to sleep before I got home, but I decided to let her sleep, and settled down on the couch. When I woke up the next morning, Mom was still lying there with all her clothes on, even her apron. I realized that she must have caught something and went to the drugstore to buy some Dispirin and Coldrex, maybe she had the 'flu. But she didn't take the tablets when I offered them to her. She kept on sleeping in that same position, and was totally quiet. She had always been a quiet one, of course, but her illness seemed to make her even quieter. I went to work, dropped by the grocery store on the way home, and prepared some simple stuff I knew how to make. I offered her some but she didn't even touch it. I kept talking to her, and after a couple of weeks she started answering, just a few words at a time, and she asked me to bathe her and to put a nightgown on her. I said all right, even though it terrified me to see her naked. I really did not want to undress her, but I had to do it. Her eyes were closed and there was a strange sweet smile on her lips. I avoided looking at her face, and she was as heavy as a sack of concrete, but I managed and went to work and waited for her to get better and for our life to return to normal. I considered calling a doctor, but then I realized they'd take her to a hospital, and I did not want them to do that. I wanted to take care of her myself, and she herself told me that she didn't need a doctor. I washed her and changed her nightgown and learned how to do the household chores. Then, one Friday, the super lets himself in with his keys and starts snooping around. He starts complaining that the neighbors are saying there is a bad smell coming out of here. So he's come to check what's going on. I realized that I hadn't aired out the place for months, so I opened the window and told him Mom was sick and that was why everything was sort of a mess. He glanced at the bed and left, but when I came home the next evening I couldn't believe it — Mom had been taken away. I had just sat down to try to figure this out when the super used his key again and came in with two cops in tow. I asked them what this was about, but they just told me to get into the patrol car with them, which I did, of course, thinking that they would take me to Mom. They drove me here and I was admitted to this ward. I still don't understand why. They are keeping me here, they won't let me go to work or even to go see Mom over there in the other ward. I just don't know what's to become of us. They won't even let us share a room. Everything is all mixed-up, and they won't let me ask Mom what to do.

(We got married on the fourteenth of November and it was all over before the end of the month. As far as I'm concerned, it was a marriage that was exactly two weeks too long.) I met him at the Pam Pam where I'd dropped in for a beer with the girls after work. He walked in the door and I just knew that this was the guy for me. Later in the evening I went to his table and told him hey, man, lets get it on. We went to my place, but then it turned out there was no way I could get the creep to leave again. The fucker velcroed himself to me on the basis of that one night. He glued himself to my bed, snored on while I went to work, and when I came home, the asshole was still flat on his face. He didn't go to work, didn't go shopping, didn't even take out the fucking garbage. I put up with all that because I sort of liked him, at least in bed, when he happened to be awake. He proposed to me a week after we'd met and I said yes because it was fucking freezing November with nothing doing, not even at the Pam Pam. So I figured that my co-workers and I would have a nice excuse to party, who cared who the guy was, I'd get married and that was that. We had the wedding at the Savoy, I wore white, we got a few presents, we got shit-faced, and everybody thought it was a blast. Then it was back to reality and the same old shit, the guy just sat around and worked on crossword puzzles and farted. I could have put up with that, too, but after we'd been married for a week the fucker started whining about his miserable childhood and his really horrible adolescence and claimed that no one cared about him and that he had no reason to go on living. I listened to that for a week, every goddamn night, always the same bullshit. And I had thought I'd gotten myself a real man. So, OK, after that first week of marriage I was a nervous wreck, and I asked myself, what am I going to do with this creep who just keeps oozing on like liquid snot? The second week he got worse, started blubbering about the death of some grandma, twenty years ago. I told him this is it, man, time to pack your bags. He pointed at his ring. I took mine off and tossed it out the window. He still wouldn't leave. I tried to drag him out into the stairwell, but the guy was so sick that I couldn't get him to move. I called the cops and told them to take him away. The cops took a look at me, then they took a look at the guy, and then they left, and I grabbed a filleting knife and stuck him a couple of times. Shit, the jerk didn't even try to defend himself, he just up and died in the only bed I have. I called Hesperia hospital and told them that my husband had committed suicide by stabbing himself in the chest, and then I went to stay with a girl I knew from work. She calmed me down and told me these things happen. We drank some coffee and went to work the next morning. That day the cops called me and asked for details. I told them everything, I said I had gone to the john to read the paper, and when I came out, the guy had killed himself. They believed every word, and the girls at work said that I had done the right thing, it was the little shit's own fault, he'd asked for it by clinging to me and whining like that. Shit, I need a real guy who takes care of things, helps pay off the mortgage, puts stuff in the refrigerator. **Hell,** if a guy wants to live with you he's got to take on some **responsibilities.**

After the funeral she locked herself in the bedroom. She did not eat, drink, or sleep for twelve days and nights. The sun rose and set but she paid no attention to it. She felt like a stranger to herself, and everything she saw and thought seemed fragmented. She did not reminisce about the past, but she could still smell her husband in the sheets of their double bed. There had been moments of happiness. There had been stout infants babbling on the living room rug on Sunday mornings, the man still sleepy next to her, she herself beautiful and fragrant in the front seat of the car on her way to work. All that had been a long time ago, or perhaps only yesterday. Either it had happened, or else it was just a fantasy.

Naked, she climbed onto the bed. She looked at herself in the mirror on the bedroom ceiling. She looked hard but could not see anything. Not even her own face. She picked a heavy vase off the floor and tossed it at the ceiling. The mirror shattered and rained down on her. The splinters tore bleeding wounds into her body. Some of the wounds were deep and gaping and blood streamed out of them. The blood soaked into the sheets, her body throbbed with heat, and the blood smelled like old, hard life. She jumped down to the floor. Mirror splinters pierced the soles of her feet but she did not feel any pain. Excited, she danced from wall to wall, humming an unknown melody. The white-flowered wallpaper became stained with red. Her breasts and thighs were steaming with blood. When she finished the dance and collapsed on the floor, the last drops of blood gathered in a puddle in her own lap.

t was past three in the morning when he opened
the nightstand drawer, took out the gun, loaded
it. The skin under his eyes was black from weeks of insom-
nia, and hard wrinkles had carved themselves into his forehead and into the corners of his eyes. The foggy light of a
streetlamp filtered through the window. It showed that the
big double bed was half empty. His wife had left him years
ago, moved to the other side of town to live with her aging
mother. He looked at the vacant street. Palmtrees, new green
grass, a stray cat on the hood of a car. He took aim at the cat,
pretended to shoot, lowered the gun again. The house had
five large, sparsely furnished rooms, Persian rugs, fresh
flower arrangements. He glanced at the door as if afraid
someone might enter. This was quite unlikely, the boy had
not visited the bedroom once after the man's sex life, minimal at best, had come to an end when his wife moved out. He
looked back into the street: the cat was gone. Everything had
really been decided, but stories he had heard as a child, about
people who had died young and whose souls couldn't find
rest, confused him for a moment. A heavy sense of sin had
bent his shoulders and back. Then he managed to detach
himself from the painful atmosphere of those old tales. He
opened the bedroom door and strode through the living
room, the dining room, the library. He stopped at the end of

the hall and felt ready to do it. He had nothing left in the world except for the boy. He could not remember a single moment of pleasure in his long life, for even in his marriage-bed the bookkeeper of sins had squatted on his shoulder and enumerated all the conceivable evil he had perpetrated against God, from original sin onwards. Quietly he stepped up to the boy's door and opened it a crack. A wave of nausea swept over him. The boy was fast asleep, a naked woman by his side. Cold shivers ran down the man's spine and spread all over his body. He looked at the woman's large breasts and painted mouth and felt more miserable than ever before these sinners adrift in their dreams. He raised the gun and took aim. Slowly he pulled the trigger, with a great sense of triumph, for only after losing everything could he face himself as a winner. Then his arm sank down and he almost dropped the gun on the floor. He was trembling, his eyes were open wide with terror, and he pulled the door shut. Tears ran down his cheeks. He wiped them off, swallowed them and the weakness he hated, went back to his bedroom, put the gun in the nightstand drawer and buried his head in a big pillow.

Her white lace blouse was dazzling, her dark curly hair precisely coiffed, and her heavy golden earrings swung as she chewed on a greasy chicken leg in the restaurant of the Viking Line ferry. She gave me a quick and penetrating glance as she pointed at the empty chair at the end of the table.

"They shot and killed my husband three years ago, in downtown Ähtäri. Shot him with a sawed-off shotgun, at such close range that the top of his head splattered all over the walls."

She takes a big bite out of a chicken breast, chews rapidly, wipes the grease off the corners of her mouth with the back of her hand.

"What a job it was to scrub the place. I tell you, girl, you can't imagine how hard it can to be get that stuff out, blood and gray matter that's dried just a little bit. It took my mom and myself two and a half days of scrubbing with baking soda and a scrubbing brush before we had the room back in some kind of shape. You can still see some stains in those pressboard walls, even after three years. Human blood makes the worst stains."

She gulps down some milk out of a large container, cleans her teeth with the nail of her little finger, looks me straight in the eye.

"Twenty-three years old I was when I became a widow. I was expecting that man's child. It was a tough time. The kid was kicking in my belly, and I had to clean up the remains of my husband. Why couldn't they at least kill him with a knife, the way they used to in the old days? It wouldn't have made such a mess. Even the dead looked better in the old days. Like my uncle, say, who was stabbed straight in the heart at the age of twenty-five. He looked so contented in his open coffin. There's no telling what my husband looked like at the moment of death. His whole head and half his chest were just raw meat."

She collects all the chicken bones into a big pile on the edge of the table and burps loudly.

There we sat, the three of us, our wrists wrapped in bandages, behind the big window, looking at the countryside around Lapinlahti, damp and spring-like green in the middle of winter. Runis had the thickest bandages, blood had kept seeping through them until this morning. I was sure he had made the deepest cut, he can never leave anything half-done. A perfectionist when it comes to pathos. Topis' face was as white as plaster of Paris, with fat purple half-moons under his eyes. He looked really terrible. His slow-motion eyes swept across the boring landscape. When his eyes met mine, he started smiling, a typical Topis smile. I smiled back. I wasn't doing so badly. I had cut one wrist open but only scratched the other one, just enough to show. I rarely go to extremes. Topis' gaze sought Runis' eyes, and when they connected, Runis laughed out loud and said well I guess we've seen enough of this. I checked the hallway to make sure the coast was clear. A couple of mad people were slinking along the walls on their way to the phone booth and back, but we knew we needn't worry about them. I got into my own clothes, pulled off the bandages, and walked out through the front door. The receptionist looked after me with the same disgusted expression she'd had when I arrived. Runis followed, Topis came last. We waited for him outside the gate under an old birchtree. Topis tried hard to look cool as he ambled out, but the result was a weird grimace. He had left one of the bandages on, the one around his left wrist, but Runis was still wearing bandages on both wrists — a good thing, too. We walked down the middle of the tree-lined drive but stepped aside when a white taxicab drove past us. The world looked totally familiar, exactly the same as last week. We went to the Shell station at Leppäsuo, had some coffee, got on the bus. We got off at Kontula and walked through the shopping mall to Vesala and Runis' crib, just as before. The kitchen table looked like a garbage dump and there were puddles of congealed blood on the floor from last week. Topis looked at me and winked. Runis was already over by the sink, fumbling for his knife. I grabbed it out of his hand. From Topis' expression I could tell he was ready. As always, I made the first cut. Just a scratch. Then Topis sliced his right wrist for real, ripped the bandage off his left wrist, and handed the knife to Runis. Runis grinned, ripped both bandages off, and cut deep into both arteries.

The tavern is shaped like a long narrow box. The small light fixtures on the walls are wreathed in dense smoke. Drunken fishermen, sailors speaking foreign tongues, and big-breasted Grade B whores sit at the bar, talking a lot, all of them as incomprehensible to each other as can be. The rest of the room is almost dark and populated by shrieking teenage car thieves, hashish peddlers, and shit-faced retired folk. Two monks in black robes walk in the door, straight-backed and dignified. One brushes the wet snow off his shoulders, the other touches the small gold crucifix that hangs around his neck as if to make sure he hasn't lost his faith. They stride up to the bar in a practiced manner and give the faded blonde behind the bar their orders for double shots of whiskey. When the drinks arrive, they take them and walk to the front of the place, past the Eskimo fishermen with the berserker tendencies. One of the monks digs out a pipe from the breast pocket of his robe, fills it and lights up, knocks back half of his drink and glances at a beer bottle flying through the air and smashing into the opposite wall. The other monk opens his mouth to say something but then closes it again and smiles quietly. They consume three more double whiskies, the smoker finishes another pipe, they leave. In the street, right in front of the bar, lies a bleeding man half-covered in wet snow. The bouncer at the door who wears leather gloves looks at the monks and says well, that's what happens to jerks who try to kick me in the balls. The monks proceed up the street to the top of a small hill from which one can see the whole town with its low buildings, all the way down to the waves of the Atlantic, just like in old photographs. They go to a five-star hotel, leave an order for breakfast and the morning papers, take the elevator to the fourth floor, and settle into their room. Slowly they take off their heavy robes and hang them up carefully on white clothes hangers. One of them cracks the seal on a bottle of Jim Beam. They sit there in their light underwear and have two more drinks each. They take a shower together and tired but content sink into the white silk sheets on the soft waterbed.

After he had thrown sand on top of the coffin in the name of the father, the son, and the holy ghost, he came into the sacristy, exchanged the priest's vestments for a black monk's robe and put on his monk's beret. He stood and smiled at me for a moment, then took a big gulp of red wine from the communion chalice and burped. We left by the back door, avoiding the pompous façade of the church. We walked through town, waded through snowdrifts, slipped in the icy courtyards. He walked half a step in front of me, the hem of his worn black robe sweeping the ground. The house was old and yellow, its concrete front steps almost hidden by a thick layer of snow. By the door he made a perfunctory sign of the cross and we went inside. Above the door hung a weatherbeaten image of God. It was cold inside. I did not take off my coat. I sat down at the kitchen table and looked out at the back yard which was littered with junk and garbage. He put on some water, went to the liquor cabinet, served me some hot rum with honey. The bedroom, behind the kitchen, had a short and narrow wooden bed, a leatherbound Bible on the nightstand, two white candles in pewter candlesticks; the walls were covered with floral wallpaper that had worn very thin, and through the small window one could see some red cars covered in snow. I got into the bed and squeezed myself under a thick, cold, and damp pile of blankets. He joined me, stroked my hair for a moment, then got under the covers without taking off his robe. We were a tight fit in that bed, the mattress was hard. He kissed my eyelids, touched my neck, and searched for my lips with his mouth. I kicked my woolen socks off my feet, he did the same. I tossed my sweater on the floor, he took off his beret. He peeled five layers of clothes off me and I was naked under the damp sheet. He did not smile but his eyes told me everything. I lit the candles. In the noonday sun, one could hardly see their flames. He got out of his pants but did not take off the robe or the heavy metal crucifix. He had long, pitch-black hair, a curly, clean, well-trimmed beard, and very white hands. He entered me. It felt worse than two switchblades in the chest. The blood flowed and I kissed him, took his pretty penis in my hand and felt it grow into a Tower of Babel between my thighs. We lay in that hard and narrow bed until the following morning. Then he had to return to the back door and the sacristy, to exchange his monk's robe for the priest's, and to throw sand on the dead.

etween the center of town and the hostel lay a large moor, frozen into a glistening ice field by the February winds blowing from the Atlantic. The woman was crossing the moor on her way back to the hostel. She wore a fur coat, tall leather boots and an angry expression. Up in the sky, a plane drew a wavy jet-trail against dark blue clouds. The woman slowed down as she approached a hedge. She felt a sting in her heart and remembered something very remote. It had been the middle of summer, there had been a thick green lawn, and a pig that had squealed under the hands of a butcher. She was able to localize that memory. It had happened elsewhere, in another country, but it was true. Now she looked sad. She pushed her hands deep into the pockets of her coat and felt the cold rise from her abdomen to her forehead.

The man behind the hedge held his breath and waited for the moment when the woman would arrive at exactly the right spot. There was fear in his eyes, and the veins at his temples were swollen. He waited a few more seconds in complete silence. Then he attacked the woman, from behind. She fell on her back and struck her head on the ice. The man's breath came in fast, irregular bursts. He had a pale, childish face, long blond hair, and wore black leather gloves. He struck her in the face, tore her fur coat open, tried to pull her pants down. The woman did not cry out but gave him an appraising look. He looked quite handsome to her. She glanced up at the sky. The white trail of the plane had disappeared, only the blue clouds remained, and so did the cold that made her nipples stiffen.

"Let's do it's where it's warm," she said to the man who was desperately tugging at her tight pants. He gave a start and stopped. He stared at her with suspicion but let go of her bleeding hands.

"I have a room. It's small, but it's warm."

He looked at her swollen lips and quickly got up off her. She staggered to her feet, buttoned her blouse, fluffed her hair, then walked on toward the hostel. The man followed, walking a couple of steps behind her.

The doorman was asleep. They went to the smallest room on the first floor and undressed, the woman smoothly, the man clumsily. She pulled the bedspread off, lay down and looked at him. There was nothing but a deep void in his eyes. The woman sighed, put her hands between her thighs, closed her eyes and arranged her features in a faint smile. Timidly, the man lay down on top of her. She stroked his shoulders. He kissed her breasts and neck and tried to enter her but couldn't manage it. She closed her eyes and swallowed. With a puppy-like sob he rolled off her. They held each other, fell asleep, and slept until morning when she had to go to work. She picked a pack of cigarettes off the table and left. Around noon, the man woke up with a start and left the room without looking back.

The monk with the mitre-shaped hat started up his silver-gray 1959 Maserati in front of the west cargo terminal of the port and headed east. In the passenger seat was a woman with an Eskimo face, slender legs, blue-black hair. They drove up a narrow and icy road that followed one bank of the fjord, stopping at quiet gas stations to drink cups of tepid coffee and smoke cigarettes. They passed trucks stinking of rotten fish, Ladas emitting big black clouds of exhaust, and GMC pick-up trucks with enormous tires that mashed the tracks in the road into a wet pulp.

The house stood by itself, far from any other dwelling, close to a deep ravine. They left the car in a heated garage by the road and walked up to the house. The monk carried four plastic shopping bags, the woman pulled a leather suitcase on wheels. There was no sign of life in the yard, but lights were on in all eight rooms of the house. The woman threw her fake leopard coat on a couch and sat down in front of a television set. The monk distributed the contents of the plastic bags on the kitchen counter, put a cassette in the Bang & Olufsen videotape player, punched a key on the remote control unit. The image was crisp, the colors were right. The woman lit a Winston and stared at the movie which had a tropical setting.

The monk put his mitre on the table next to the couch,

hung his robe in the closet and put on a pair of Zic-Zac sweatpants and a t-shirt with a number on the front and the words Public Enemy on the back. Then he strolled back to the kitchen, turned on the Philips De Luxe microwave and got busy with the appliances manufactured by Moulinex, Krups, Miele and Zanussi. A tape rapped out of the Cool Key boombox on top of the Rosenlew refrigerator, the sound blending pleasantly with the jungle noises of the video. He laid the kitchen table with black plates and went down to the cellar to return with two bottles of Aloxe Corton '78.

The woman approached the table lazily. The monk held a chair for her. The video kept on running but the Cool Key was turned off.

"That kind of naïvely theistic concept of the deity provides no answers to the existential questions of postmodern woman," said the woman and took a bite of sirloin steak.

"I have tried to find an answer in contemplation," said the monk, trying to catch her eye, but she stared down at the rare steak.

"If it works for you."

After the meal, the monk put the dishes in the Zanussi dishwasher and washed and polished the Krups mixer, the Moulinex food processor, the Miele eggbeater, and the espresso machine. When he was done straightening up the kitchen, he stuck an unopened bottle of Puttony Tokay '56 under his arm and proceeded to the living room where the woman lay sleeping on the couch under her fur coat. He switched off the hissing video player, sank into an armchair, and sat there until five a.m. with a glumly contemplative expression.

ate that night I went downtown to look for Nick Cave but encountered someone quite different — a ruddy, shiny-faced fisherman from the east coast. I undressed him, talked to him long and eloquently about love, the stars, and earth's gravity. He listened to me with his big ears, smiling an innocent, idiotic smile. He wanted a lot and wanted it fast. I gave him of my best. In the morning, in the noisy double bed in the hotel, he babbled like a baby that has just been fed and wants more. I did what he wanted, smiled and whispered things into his ear, gave him the V.I.P. treatment. I let him get inside me and at that instant grabbed his neck and squeezed as hard as I was able. A groan, and life slid out of the fat body. I got up, put on my clothes, ordered breakfast and left.

Good Friday, and church bells clattered in the streets of the small fishing village. At the cannery hostel, in its communal kitchen, a Moroccan unwrapped an Easter egg covered with gold foil. The hostel was empty and quiet. The man took a bite out of the chocolate egg, set it on the table, glanced at his wristwatch. He crumpled the gold foil, tossed it into the garbage and walked across the hall to his room. Everything looked ready : the gray, torn robe on the armchair, the executioner's hood on the bed, two rags for his feet. He put on the robe and the hood and checked in the mirror that the hood was attached properly. Then, carefully, he tied the rags over his black leather shoes and went down the hall. By the front door stood a cross made out of styrofoam, crudely painted to look like wood. He put the cross on his shoulder and walked quickly down the street to the small harbor where the procession was to begin. There was no one at all in the harbor. The man looked around, smoked a cigarette, and spat before setting out again. Large white flocks of gulls circled above, flying low but not screeching. The cross bounced on the man's shoulder. The weather was sunny and calm. The man walked with a heavy stride, his back bent, his eyes downcast. Now people rushed out of their houses and the air reverberated with their screaming and wailing. The gulls screeched, the women squealed like pigs about to be butchered, the men waved their arms as if reaching for the last rope of salvation lowered down from the heavens. The children's faces looked curiously distorted. The man staggered on, stumbled over the tattered hem of his robe, fell to the ground with the cross on top of him. Out of the crowd emerged a man in a blue suit and white shirt who was wiping tears off his cheeks while hastening to assist the cross-bearer. He, too, shouldered the cross, pretending to reel under its weight. The crowd followed the two cross-bearers. Lamentations echoed from the frozen mountainsides. They proceeded the six hundred yards to the church where the crowd was left milling around on the steps : only the hooded man was allowed in. When the man in the blue suit, now wearing the expression of a Good Samaritan, had closed the door behind the man and his cross, the crowd fell silent. Its members dried their tears and hurried back to their homes, laughing and joking, ready for the baked lamb that was waiting for them. Inside the church, the man tossed the cross into a corner of the vestibule, walked up to the pulpit and took off his hood and robe. Then he went to the lavatory, combed a little gel into his hair, and walked back to the hostel in his bluejeans and brown leather jacket. He sat down at the kitchen table and enjoyed the second half of his chocolate egg.

There were five men around the table. The oldest took out a deck of cards carved out of whalebone and dealt. No one said anything. The men played a fast game, none of them looked at the others. Their faces were serious and the tobacco smoke in the room was dense. The pot grew after each round. The old man kept losing as he always did, not because he wasn't a good player but because he no longer knew his place. Once he had been a prince, now he was a pauper. He glanced at the others, young men with their lives before them, radiant with strength, health, and greed. The old man knew that by the end of the last round he would have lost everything and would then be another person. His last banknotes found their way into other men's pockets. The young men did not smile, even though they had reason to, but retained a serious and respectful expression. The lights went out, the men left the room. The night air felt heavy and humid. They walked down the slushy street, heading for the center of town, each one of them pondering his winnings and losses. The old man fell behind. It was easy for him to do, he had lost the most. The broad shoulders and strong arms of the young men made him feel even more inadequate. He touched the pistol tucked inside his waistband, lit a cigarette, smoked it, and carefully pulled the gun. No one noticed anything. He shot all four of them in the back. They fell down in the street, their blood tinting the slush red. The old man walked up to the bodies. The holes in their backs looked very modest and small. He made sure all of them were dead and put the muzzle of the gun in his mouth.

While the warriors at the base were putting on their leather suits and flying boots, the man came home, took off his big frilly collar, put it on the kitchen table, and kissed the woman who never smiled. She sat on a stool next to the freezer, staring at the man. He proffered a handful of bright yellow pills. She swallowed them in a practiced manner. She was exceptionally pretty, young, and neurotic. The man took a lunchbox out of the freezer, went to the closet to get a flashlight, put both things into a small backpack. Then he placed a narrow leather collar around the woman's neck, attached a long gold-plated leash to the collar, and locked the other end of the leash to the handle of the freezer. With attentive eyes, the woman followed his every move. The man took three small bottles out of his pocket and carefully arranged three rows of pills on the windowsill, wagged his finger at her, grabbed the backpack off the floor and left. He had to reach the edge of the glacier before dusk. After the sound of his footsteps had faded in the street, the woman got off the stool. She held the chain, looked up at the narrow strip of sky and wondered who that stranger in black was who would visit her apartment and her life, a strange man wearing a white ruff who came rarely and left frequently. Perhaps he was an alien from the Third Milky Way, a well-meaning angel who had assumed the shape of a devil. The thought calmed her down, and while she let her heavy eyelids droop and felt very happy, fifteen gray-green reconnaissance helicopters swept across the sky. They formed a silent plow that moved rapidly toward the east and cast a dark, bird-shaped shadow over the town below.

I met him at six in the morning, at a bus stop on the edge of town. He was black. He had his belongings in five large plastic bags and carried a long drum. He wanted to know if I was going to the east coast. We sat on our bags in the light sleeting rain and smoked imported American cigarettes. The bus arrived two hours late. He was from the savannahs of Central Africa, somewhere near Zaïre. He had crossed the Atlantic on a boat a week ago, and he intended to stay, although he wasn't able to explain why. We spent eleven drowsy hours on the bus, riding through blizzards, rain, sunshine and snowdrifts. Late at night we arrived in a small port town. Its main street was empty, the display windows were dark. The only lit-up thing we saw was an oil company's gigantic billboard blazing on the mountainside. We found a room for the night behind the cannery. It had a big window, wall-to-wall carpeting with bug stains, and two iron-framed beds. In the morning we went to the cannery, but they had no work for us. He was too black and too primitive-looking, and I bet I was turned away because I came with him. For three days we sat on our beds, wrapped in many layers of blankets, drinking instant coffee and rolling cigarettes. He found the landscape depressing. It consisted of frozen heaps of stone. He longed for the African sun. I forgot the past and let the future take care of itself. On the morning of the fourth day, we took the bus back to the capital. An electric blue sun shone above the Atlantic, and I knew there would be a change in my life.

After adjusting the focus, he snapped the picture. A moment later the camera spat out a black square of paper. He handed it to her with a smile.

"Just wait a minute."

She tossed her curly mane and looked at the black piece of paper with suspicion.

"It's developing. You'll see."

She looked at him with a doubtful expression, then stared at the black square.

"Did I look good?"

"You looked great," he said and licked his dry lips.

Silence. Her small black bikini showed off her coffee-brown breasts, small flat stomach, and almost non-existent buttocks. It was obvious to everyone on the beach that he had the hots for her. She shifted her weight from one foot to the other, looked glum.

"I don't think this is going to make it. It's still black."

"I guess not," he said, took the piece of paper from her and tossed it on the sand. She took his hand, and together they ran along the beach all the way to the rocks at the far end, where they stopped, out of breath, laughed and kissed.

After all the people had left the beach, a young girl wearing a white sweater came walking and found the picture. You could see the blue sea and a pretty small-breasted woman in a black bikini. The woman was smiling. The girl looked at the print for a long time, feeling curiously aroused. Without hesitating, she stuck the print in her skirt pocket and walked back home. There she sat quietly until her father turned off the television and her mother flushed the toilet. She undressed, took the picture of the woman from under the mattress, and kissed it.

She came to town a week ago but I haven't seen her yet. I don't know why I don't want to meet her. I stay away from the city center, I don't go out in the evenings, I avoid the streets and the bars because I don't want to run into her. I see her as an intruder in my country and my city. This is the only world I have, and I don't want her to come and make a mess of everything. She rang my doorbell. I did not go to the door but I did not turn the lights out either. She could tell I was here. Then a note dropped through the mail slot, with the name of a hotel and a phone number. I looked at it for a long time before I tossed it into the waste basket. It has been three years since I left her. I wanted to be a cowboy who leaves without saying goodbye while implying that he might return. I did not intend to return then, nor do I intend to do so now. I left her because I wanted to live by myself. I don't like the odors of other people, I don't like unexpected facial expressions, I don't like the way they pose at dinner tables or in front of television sets. I want to live by myself because I don't need anybody, least of all a woman who turns everything into a problem. Yet I sit here in this armchair in a cramped basement room for six days, thinking about her all the time. I don't have a moment's peace because I can't think about anything but her. I am so excited I can't sleep. I can feel my pulse beating in my head and in my fingertips. I am excited by the knowledge that she is in town, in a nearby hotel, while I am down here in this stifling cellar. It would easy for me to get some relief by just unzipping my pants and jacking off, but I won't do that. I want to torture myself for as long as she stays in town. I want to enjoy every second. I torment myself by staying excited and will relent only after she has flown back to her country of origin.

The man sits in a naugahyde easy chair, in a living room brightly lit by a fluorescent tube. The dusty china objects on top of the bookshelf by the back wall cannot compete with the sharply defined image on the television screen. It is an hour past midnight, and the man is only pretending to watch what is on. A red light comes through the window and moves past the doorway toward the cheap landscape painting on the wall. The man shifts in his chair. This does not relieve the tension in his muscles. He picks the remote control off the floor and switches the image to that of a dark-skinned woman who is pushing a yard-long cucumber into her vagina. The man raises his hand and fondles his limp member. The expression on the video woman's face is blissful, her mouth is a moaning O. The man feels how his member stiffens inside his polyester sweatpants and soon reaches its full dimensions. He gulps and glances at the bedroom door. It is white and it is closed. He turns back to the screen and grabs the black woman's huge breasts with his stare. He puts his hand inside his pants and takes hold of his stiff member, slaps it against his flabby belly, keeps an eye on the bedroom door. The black woman sucks the last inch of cucumber into herself and groans, the man pumps frantically, he looks frightened, the naugahyde chair creaks. Now the black woman on the screen has been replaced by a white male trudging through a dense African jungle. The man tucks his soft wet dick back into his pants, holds his breath for a moment, then switches the TV off. He remains in the chair for a while and feels how peace spreads through his muscles from head to heel. The red light has passed the tacky landscape and advances toward the armchair. The man yawns, gently strokes his belly and his flabby breasts, gets up and walks to the bedroom door, opens it quietly, and disappears into the cool but summery dark.

took the early flight to Helsinki and bought myself a guy right there at the airport. He had brown eyes and broad shoulders but was perhaps a tad overweight. His face was acceptable, and it wore a fairly boyish expression. He wasn't exactly what I would have liked, but he had a dick. We went to a hotel and I made him work for his pay. I lay on my back, I got down on all fours, I leaned on the table, I sat on the couch, I stood up against the wall. Then I paid him, gave him a nice tip, and sent him packing. I took a hot bubble bath and called room service to order some women's magazines and a bottle of champagne. I read the magazines and slowly finished the bottle. I got dressed and went to the seminar at Otaniemi. I stayed there for two hours, signed the register, smiled at the supervisor. Then I took in a play, had a drink at a nightclub after that, and returned to the hotel for a good night's sleep in the soft wide double bed.

The next morning I flew home and told my husband that it had just been another working trip. He believed me.

picked her up at the Fennia Bar. She wore a
shabby skirt and a cheap t-shirt that left nothing
to the imagination. She took me home and treated me like I
was the gold medalist at the national dog show. I enjoyed
that. An old urban cowboy like me really deserves that kind
of care. Let me tell you, I've been through more than the rest
of the inhabitants of the Hanko peninsula put together. I've
slept in dumps no one else would even consider, I've spent
years in smoky greasy spoons, I've downed beers by the
case. Summers I've slept with my boots on in Sinebrychoff
Park, feeding on hot dogs in abandoned railroad stations.
I've been reduced to raping little girls in Kaisaniemi Park
during the worst freeze the south has known. So I had really
earned that woman's tender loving care. Sixteen weeks is a
good time. Enough to put a man back on his feet, no matter
what shape he's in. I left her with money in my pocket and
my backpack full of provisions. She and her three children
smiled and waved goodbye from their nice Finnish fifth-
floor balcony.

"I got tired of people, tired of the world. Tired of the pointless noise, the shouting at the stock exchange, the innocent young bankers and insurance company men who always want something from you."

The men sit in silence for a moment on the small black leather couch in the middle of a bright room with a high ceiling. They face a clear view of Manhattan's tall buildings ascending up into the thick cloud layer in the sky.

"I lived one life there, another life here. *There*, there was too much of everything — here, there isn't enough of anything, and that's great. When I came here, I rented this hotel room and decided to love only myself. I didn't give anyone my address. I have been able to live in total isolation from the outside world, and I am happier than I have ever been. The world and its people have remained at exactly the right distance."

The man in the blue suit gets off the couch and walks over to the window. For a long while he stares down at the crowded street, its streetlights and neon, where black people gather discarded newspapers to use as blankets and pale Indians in doorways stick needles into their arms.

"There, I tried to meet every demand that was made on me. I was a perfect worker, husband, lover, patriarch. I was perfect even when I was asleep. But no one can keep that up forever. And that is why I came here."

The men toast each other, for old friendship's sake, and exchange pained grins. The only sound in the room is the even hum of the efficient air-conditioner. The man in blue unbuttons the top button of his shirt, loosens the knot of his tie. He misses his home, he misses the embrace of his wife, the familiar breakfast table.

"Here, I give myself everything. I serve and worship myself the way I once served those who were ready to take everything but were never willing to give."

The man in the blue suit feels depressed and utterly empty. For a moment he thinks about the life he would have liked to lead, glances at the other man, clears his throat.

"I've always . . . ," he starts, but the words stick in his throat.

The other man looks up from the white wall-to-wall carpeting and uses the remote control to turn on the football game.

She was sitting in the kitchen, the young lady with the pouty lips, and before I was able to make it to the door, she pounced on me. All right, I said to myself, so maybe this is that cool blonde I've always dreamed about meeting at a party. She said she was from some small town. Pink skin, built like a fashion model. She wanted to dine in style, so we did. My treat, of course. Then she wanted to see my apartment and its great sea views, so she called a cab, which I paid for. In the back seat, she leaned her head against my shoulder and giggled just like a small town girl. She drank my Scotch, she smoked my last cigarette, she turned off the record player in the middle of my favorite piece. She checked out all my kitchen appliances and polished off a jar of caviar with her fingers. Then she lounged on my leather couch in her miniskirt and tried to look really mature. When she finally drawled out her request that I carry her to the waterbed and screw her, I was completely turned off. I told her look here, young lady, isn't it enough that I've paid for your entire evening's entertainment? I'm no goddamn sex object. I made her sit on the afghan rug in the lotus position and gave her a nine-hour lecture on Taoism. It was all way over her pretty Barbie Doll head, but I didn't let her go. I told her I had a right to get something in return for the money I'd spent on her. I let her go the next day, after one o'clock. She was really freaked out. She ran to the bus stop as if pursued by some murderous rapist and shouted over her shoulder that I was the most perverse asshole she had ever met.

hey released me on Friday morning. They gave me a train ticket and I made it to Helsinki well before noon. I took the streetcar to a Mercedes dealership on Mannerheimintie. They let me take the latest model for a test drive. I drove to Vuosaari, to Paula's place, and let myself in with my own key. I grabbed a carton of milk from the fridge and knocked it back. Then I called Paula at work, and she knew right away that I was in Vuosaari. She took a cab and got there in no time. We made coffee, Paula fixed some toasted sandwiches, and we screwed in the armchair. Paula was giggly like she always is when she sees me. It had been a while, three months at least, and you could tell: I was horny, and she was, too. Paula stuffed some underwear and a black evening gown into a bag and got into the passenger seat, proud as a peacock. Then we took off. She complimented me on my taste. She likes big white cars. I drove to the Casino in Katajanokka, made sure no one was in, broke the kitchen window, and ambled over to the bar. I collected twenty bottles of Scotch from the bar and another ten from the cooler. Then some Bacardi rum, brandy, five cases of beer, and a case of Finncream for Paula. I put all that in the trunk, and then we started out for Lohja. The sun was shining bright, it was just a couple of degrees below freezing, and we stopped at the best hotel off the freeway for

Chateaubriand steaks with mashed potatoes. I had remembered to bring a bottle of wine from the Casino, and we dined like lords. I was a free man, I had the world's sweetest lady by my side, I had a car and a trunkload of booze. Paula took care of the bill and we drove on to Turku. We took a suite at the Seurahuone, brought some booze in, had some drinks. This was the life. I had a few Napoleon brandies, Paula had Pepsis with Bacardi. I screwed Paula every which way. Then we had something to eat, then we screwed some more. Paula has a dynamite body, boobs you wouldn't believe. The next morning we pushed on to Jyväskylä. In that crate you could do a hundred and twenty, easy, and we had drinks all the way. In Jyväskylä, we took a room at the Cumulus but couldn't stand it there for more than a couple of hours. We screwed, had something to eat, then drove on to Oulu. By the time we got there we were really wiped out. I parked right in front of the Vaakuna, and we went up to the ninth floor. We ordered the best room service had to offer but fell asleep before they brought it to us. On Sunday we burnt rubber back to Helsinki. Paula had overcharged her Visa card by a couple of thousand, and I knew it was time to sell the Mercedes. I zipped over to Lehtisaari and sold the white dream — didn't get much for it, but it was ready cash. The buyer didn't even ask for papers. He bought it because the price was right. I have to admit that he was already half-crocked, there in the Golden Bull bar where we made the transaction. He really got it for a song, but I'm a generous guy, I don't begrudge another businessman his dream. Then we took the plane to Joensuu where we engaged in some more bedroom athletics. Man, that woman has an incredible body. Then it was Monday morning, and Paula flew back to Helsinki to work. I stayed in Joensuu for a day to rest up. Monday night I took the plane to Helsinki where the cops had a welcoming committee for me at the airport. I was a little surprised but didn't ask any questions, they must have had their reasons for taking me straight to Pasila. There, I slept for a few days. I was pretty worn out after screwing her fifteen times a day and getting hardly any sleep. I could really use that rest. Then Paula came to see me and told me what was up. Everything would have been OK if I hadn't been so generous as to leave the booze in the trunk of the Mercedes. The guy opens it and realizes that he hasn't only bought a car but also what seems to be the inventory of a liquor store in a mid-sized Finnish town. He gets worried and calls the cops, telling them that some maniac must have stuffed the trunk of his car with all this booze. He's suffering from an infernal hangover and can't even stand the idea of liquor, that morning. So. There's prints all over the car, mine and Paula's. The cops let themselves into her apartment that evening while she's already in bed and fast asleep. They take Paula's purse and figure out our weekend itinerary. They find her last flight ticket stub, it says Joensuu to Helsinki. So, that was that weekend. Paula managed to screw me in the visitation room, and things don't look so bad at all. We agreed to pick up where we left off, soon as I get out of here again.

Also published by Serpent's Tail

Sex and the City
Marsha Rowe (ed.)

'Unerringly entertaining and thought provoking.'
JOANNA BRISCOE, *Girl About Town*

'The whole book opens into the category of good dirty fun, and is not the worse for that.'
ROBERT NYE, *The Guardian*

'A mixture of 1980s eroticism, sexual humiliation and an underlying wistful longing for the milk of human kindness, seemingly destroyed by urban living. Compulsive stuff.'   *The List*

'Strangely intriguing.'   *Glasgow Herald*

'There is no other collection quite like *Sex and the City*.'   *TES*

Also published by Serpent's Tail

The Piano Teacher
Elfriede Jelinek

'A bravura performance.'

SHENA MACKAY, *Sunday Times*

'Good books, like haircuts, should fill you with awe, change your life, or make you long for another. Elfriede Jelinek's *The Piano Teacher* manages to fulfil at least two of these demands in a reckless recital that is difficult to read and difficult to stop reading. The racy, relentless, consuming style is a metaphor for passion: impossible to ignore.'

CAROLE MORIN, *New Statesman & Society*

'Something of a land-mine . . . a brilliant, deadly book.' ELIZABETH J. YOUNG, *City Limits*

'Some may see, in the pain of this novel, its panic and its deep despair, a model of current writing. For others, *The Piano Teacher* will remain a perverse horror story of a mother's love taken to its logical, deadly extreme.'

ANGELA MCROBBIE, *The Independent*

Wonderful, Wonderful Times
Elfriede Jelinek

"Spartan . . . dry and laconic."   *TLS*

"Brilliant . . . undeniably powerful . . . Jelinek's fear of decay, decline and death, is described in a simultaneously brutal and subtle poetic flow."

New Statesman

"An astonishing novel . . . a unique voice . . . truly essential reading."   *Blitz*

"Undeniably gripping."   *Time Out*

"Jelinek's writing is careful and intense."

New York Newsday

"Jelinek's characters, and the voice she uses to tell of them, are fashioned with black irony and jarring distortion. Yet the ultimate effect is grace, a dark image delivered in terms appropriate to it, but in a draftsmanship that conveys a hint of delicacy and lyricism, as if these had been ejected from the room but continued to haunt it."   *LA Times*

"Sometimes painful, sometimes ludicrously comic in tone . . . a brilliant if grim exploration of fascism. Clearly sympathetic to socialism and feminism, Jelinek nevertheless has no political axe to grind in particular . . . Her goal is to examine society with a cool, analytical eye. Youth, love, art, political systems, memory, religion, intellectualism and even nature are placed on the Jelinek operating table and stripped of all our most treasured notions."

The Nation

Winter's Child
Dea Trier Mørch

'You can almost smell the heavy perfume of birth, a mixture of blood and sweet milk. Evocative and powerful writing, it rings true to women's experience.' SHEILA KITZINGER

'Simply wonderful.' *City Limits*

'How I wish that *Winter's Child* had been written [when I was pregnant]... I came away from this book with a clearer perception of my own experience.'

Women's Review

Illustrated by the author

Evening Star

'This is a remarkable novel, dealing squarely and unsentimentally with death.' *Sunday Times*

'Superbly illustrated by the author's own woodcuts, which are simple and black and bear a kind of dignified beauty amply in keeping with the mood of this book.' *City Life*

Illustrated by the author

The Seven Deadly Sins
Alison Fell (ed.)

'Seven fine writers, seven vices probed to the quick. Splendid.' ANGELA CARTER

'These seven writers represent . . . a newer and more knowing feminist strategy . . . Mischievous and exhilarating.' LORNA SAGE, *The Observer*

'Rich in experiment and imagination, a sign of just how far contemporary women's writing might go.' HELEN BIRCH, *City Limits*

'All of these stories cut deeply and with a sharp edge into the main business of life — death, God and the devil.' RICHARD NORTH, *New Musical Express*

'A rich but random survey of recent women's writing.' JONATHAN COE, *The Guardian*

'An exciting, imaginative mix of stories.' ELIZABETH BURNS, *The List*

'Witty, modern, female.' KATHLEEN JAMIE, *Scotland on Sunday*

'Extremely entertaining.' EMMA DALLY, *Cosmopolitan*

Border Lines
Stories of Exile and Home
edited by Kate Pullinger

In these stories, 'home' is not a place, but a state of mind. Through dislocations, emigration and immigration, enforced exile and language confusion, the characters in these stories try to make a place for themselves. *Border Lines* moves from Texas to England, from Canada to New Zealand, from India to Paris, from Guyana to Brazil. It is anchored nowhere except in the imaginativeness, wit and energy of the individual stories.

Ready to Catch Him Should He Fall
Neil Bartlett

'Ceremonial, sumptuous, perverse, this novel is a compendium of a century of gay experience ... *Ready to Catch Him Should He Fall* is both journalism and fairy tale – and the best gay book of the year.'

EDMUND WHITE

'Bartlett's whirling, clotted style picks up references from Wilde and Genet, Hollywood and blues songs, to throw up freshly lyrical landscapes of lust.'

Daily Telegraph

'A triumph both in its execution and its intent.'

Sunday Times

'As good a novel as you are likely to read this year ... A writer who can really change the way people think.' *Literary Review*

320 pages (paper)

Dreaming of Dead People
Rosalind Belben

This is an intimate portrait of a woman approaching middle-age, lonely, starved of love, yet avoiding the seductions of resentment. First published ten years ago and now reissued in paperback by Serpent's Tail, *Dreaming of Dead People* is a joyful, stark novel by one of the most distinctive voices of contemporary fiction.

'Rosalind Belben's eye for the movement and texture of the natural world is extraordinarily acute and she has a poet's ear for language. Her book, although apparently a cry of loneliness and deprivation, is also a confession of fulfilment, of endless curiosity for, and love of, life.' SELINA HASTINGS, *Daily Telegraph*

'[Belben's] heroine is a solitary woman who is suffering as she reconciles herself to loneliness and sterility. She tells of her past and recalls, often, the countryside, where being alone is not painful and, if there is no meaning to life, the call to the senses is immediate.' HILARY BAILEY,*The Guardian*

'So extraordinarily good that one wants more, recognizing a writer who can conjure an inner life and spirit, can envisage, in unconnected episodes, a complete world: one unified not by external circumstances but by patterns of the writer's mind.'
ISABEL QUIGLY, *Financial Times*

Also published by Serpent's Tail

Is Beauty Good
Rosalind Belben

'A startling record of life preserved in the face of increasing desolation . . . Rosalind Belben's gift or burden is to press on to the painful edge of what is possible. It is an achievement to celebrate.'

MAGGIE GEE, *The Observer*

'In her work Belben gives us glimpses of such beauty that one can only choose, like her, to celebrate life.'

LINDA BRANDON, *The Independent*

'Spare, lucid prose, reminiscent of Woolf's *The Waves.*'   *The Guardian*

'Belben has an ability to tap deeply into the process of thought itself with all its fragmentation, puns, jokes, obscenities and moments of transfiguration . . . In this case beauty is certainly good.'

ELIZABETH J. YOUNG, *City Limits*